# A WAYFARER

## AND THE

# OWLS

## A DYSTOPIAN NOVEL

## Micah Keiser

WESTBOW
PRESS®

A DIVISION OF THOMAS NELSON
& ZONDERVAN

WestBow Press books may be ordered through booksellers or by contacting:

WestBow Press
A Division of Thomas Nelson & Zondervan
1663 Liberty Drive
Bloomington, IN 47403
www.westbowpress.com
844-714-3454

ISBN: 979-8-3850-2274-8 (sc)
ISBN: 979-8-3850-2276-2 (hc)
ISBN: 979-8-3850-2275-5 (e)

Library of Congress Control Number: 2024906856

Print information available on the last page.

WestBow Press rev. date: 7/31/2024

Special thanks to Joel and Robyn Keiser, and Jan Lynn
for your honesty and time spent reading my book and
for all the conversations relating to this book.

# CONTENTS

## CHAPTER 1

# A PRETTY LITTLE TOWN

The village of Christville is described by three words: neat, clean, and quiet. At the center of this quiet, petite city stands Christville Church. The church has white siding and a gray shingled roof. Two sets of double doors extend from the front of the church. Two clear half-circle windows hang above the double doors. Two extensions spread from the left and right and join the wall of the worship sanctuary on one side. They enclose staircases into the basement, which open into one large room with several smaller rooms surrounding it.

The large basement room is used for big social gatherings. Some of the smaller rooms are used for the Sunday school, others for storage. The church's offices and meeting room are located here as well. The sanctuary is the largest part of the building. It extends two stories into the air at its highest point. Eight large Greek style, stained glass windows that detail different scenes from the Bible line both sides of the worship sanctuary.

Each part of the church intersects at a tall white steeple with a large bell that has not been used in quite some time. The bell permanently resides in a high-reaching belfry. The outlines of three extravagant windows are carved into the right, left, and front of the steeple. A small cross is at the top of the steeple like a great bird nesting at the tallest height. The church holds the status of the tallest building in Christville.

The commercial and business buildings that comprise downtown Christville sprawl around the church like a defensive perimeter. This town has many standard businesses to serve the public, including a bank, a grocery store, and a clothing store. The buildings vary in size. For example, the diner only has one floor while the clothing store has three. However, every building is painted white. Some have bricks while others use siding. Many incorporate different colors in their trim. The alleys are slightly overgrown but otherwise retain a clean and tidy appearance. A construction contractor resides in Christville to undertake large building projects to keep them to Christville code.

The residential neighborhoods are situated around the business district. Each house is painted that same universal white with diverse exceptions on the trim, porch, or shutters. The majority are two-story farmhouses seen in small towns with lengthy histories. Every house has a neat lawn, a pretty fence surrounding it, and a tidy, weed-free garden in the backyard. An infinite forest surrounds Christville on the north, east, and west.

Christville's economic lifelines to the world are its numerous hiking trails that lead to the multifamily lodge on the northern side of town. A meat processing plant is located on the south side of Christville. Aside for its intended purpose, it also opens its doors to the hunters and processes the animals they killed in the forest. The residents say this is a major convenience.

There is also a tree farm and lumbermill in the northwest. Its employees are active in tree harvesting, cutting, and planting. It is one of the busiest businesses in the area. The lumbermill business is the pride and joy of its employees, and they guard the trees from tree poachers.

Besides the meat plant, the southern side of Christville is dominated by its school and the well-maintained vacant lot behind it. This field gives way to more woods with complementing sections of fallow ground. A winding river meanders through the northeast corner, causing several hidden ponds, streams, and fountains.

A small road curves through the southeast away from Christville to the outside world. That road is the only way for cars to travel to Christville, and Christville's businesses need it to survive. The road is well traveled, and the construction contractor makes sure it is well maintained.

The forests to the south and parts of the east are owned by Christville's inhabitants, while the forests to the west are occupied by the lumber company and the hiking and camping grounds, referred to as "public land" by residents, take up most of the land in the north. A sizeable section of land to the east is set aside for deer to breed, and no hunting of any type is tolerated there. Gun control advocates despise the number of firearms each family owns. Environmentalists are shocked at the number of trees felled every year and the number of animals killed during the various hunting seasons. Hunting has been the most popular sport since the first pioneers built the first log cabins and purchased the land from the Native Americans centuries ago. As a result, every boy hones his skill with a rifle.

Just as the buildings revolve around the church, so do the people's lives. While the mayor of the town captains its economic interests, the town's morality is championed by a group of older men referred to as the Owls. The town might operate under US law, but Christville's law only has one segment. Never do anything that would displease the Owls. Anaeus Armstrong is the accountant for Christville church. As a result, he has become a prominent member of these elites. There is also Titus Fox, the head pastor of Christville Church, and three other older men. The first is Oceanus Finch, who owns the meat processing facility. Then there is his brother, Gregory, a well-respected gentleman who oversees tree harvesting at the lumbermill. Josephus Spry is the last Owl. He comes from an old and distinguished family. These are the Owls.

Each Owl presides over the local government, and to the people of Christville, their wisdom easily outmatches Solomon. Their beliefs are rigid, and their wisdom stems from the Bible. They study the Scriptures daily, and they memorize and review chapters of the Bible for ready use in discussion with friends and family. This creates a flowery, old-fashioned style of speech as Scripture verses mix with their regular conversation.

The Owls have many duties in the governance of Christville. Their first task is to preside over a court where they resolve occasional disputes and mediate the rarer criminal and civil infractions.

CHAPTER 2

# THE BRONZE OWL

In the tranquil town of Christville stands a large white two-story farmhouse with black shingles and green shutters. At the back of this house, a large picture window overlooks the woods dressed in its summer green. The sheet of glass protects from the outside elements a spacious and comfortable parlor with many restful places to sit. White wallpaper with extravagant red, yellow, and blue flowers covers the walls, which are lined with antique artifacts from times long past. The floor is simple wood panel.

An idle fireplace at one end of the room witnesses the events of each day. Meanwhile, a grand couch governs from the opposite side. A stuffed rocking chair guards the entrance to the room like a gatekeeper. It retains the bad habit of thumping into the wall behind it, making it the most disagreeable object in the room. Across from the rocking chair, a straight-backed chair stands like a stately chief. All these furnishings mirror the characteristics of the room's occupants.

First, an older gentleman marches into the room with a stylish, pretentious gait. He sits in the straight-backed chair for reasons relating to his preference. To accompany his businesslike appearance, he carries a large wooden cane and wears an ornate suit the color of a moonless midnight. A small pair of spectacles are perched in the front pocket of his suit, supported by a fine golden chain. What hair he has peeks out from under the bowler hat he routinely wears, and it is as white as Santa Claus's hair. His expression radiates confidence like a perfume. His gaunt face with has deep wrinkles but not a whisker. His name is Anaeus Armstrong.

Next, a calm, motherly figure, younger than Anaeus strides into the room and sits in the discredited rocking chair with the battered wall behind it. Although she is approaching her thirty-second birthday, her youthful appearance is like an old friend. Her skin is tan from the warm weather and is smooth to both touch and appearance. Her hair is thick and springy, and colored dark brown. Her experience as a mother has bestowed upon her ears that are sharper than knives and brown, discerning eyes. Her pink dress is of a simple design with a white apron tied overtop. Her name is Annemarie Rogers. She is Anaeus's daughter, except Annemarie's last name has been changed through her happy marriage to Sheldon Rogers.

Finally, another female trots into the room and sits in the center of the couch. She is the youngest of the trio by three decades, her age barely amounts to thirteen years. Her hair is a shiny brown hue, and she wears it in a long braid that hangs down her back like a thick rope. Her dress is a fashion frozen in time. It is white and decorated with orange and purple flowers and green stems and leaves. It envelops her like the sea. She relishes her position on the poufy couch by emphatically putting one arm on each of the armrests despite the fact her slight figure awkwardly accommodates the reach. Her name is Mary Rogers, and she is Annemarie's second oldest daughter.

Once the trio selects their seats and Mary retracts her arms from the armrests to a restful position on her lap, Anaeus begins to speak.

"Your oldest daughter should deeply consider coming out of her worldly lifestyle and becoming a lady of character, for as Scripture says, 'Misfortunes pursue the sinner, but prosperity is righteousness's reward,'[1] says Anaeus in a commanding tone that accompanies one of his age and stature.

"She reminds me of when I was her age. I liked survival challenges in the woods, but I left that life behind when I grew older. This is a phase. She'll grow out of it. Besides, she knows a great deal about housekeeping, and she is a stronger Christian than you give her credit for. Therefore, I must consider her education complete. As for her actions, those are her choices. I can only show her the right way to go," Annemarie responds.

"I don't want what happened to you to happen to your daughter. That is why I don't want your daughter in the forest. I want her to stay in Christville,".

"She'll never outgrow whatever phase she is stuck in while hanging with boys," interjects Mary, not wanting to be left out of the conversation.

Annemarie glares at her sternly, and the victim of that gaze withdraws her theory.

"Make sure she receives the education I expect. You know the rules regarding a women's duties, Annemarie. Young women are not permitted in the forest or to perform any other strenuous outdoor activities. Your eldest daughter is in clear, wanton violation. If you will not do something about this, I will," Anaeus warns.

Annemarie opens her mouth to protest, but Anaeus, hand raised to silence her, interrupts, "You, on the other hand, were an exception. You broke the rules the same as your daughter has. Frankly, you got off easy."

Annemarie shifts uncomfortably in the rocking chair. With his relational business completed, Anaeus stands to leave. Calmly but imperiously, he steps out of the room, leaving Annemarie grumbling while Mary watches the door, searching for any obscure scraps of discourse. As the parlor door closes, a bronze owl that resides above

---

[1] Proverbs 13:21.

the doorframe suddenly tumbles off its perch and lands with a metallic *clang*!

"I'll get that, Mother," says Mary, hastening to reinstate the fallen owl.

Annemarie stands in the doorway and shakes her head as she watches Mary lift the owl back to its pedestal. She is already dreading the upcoming conversations today.

CHAPTER 3

# THE WAYFARER

During the meeting between Anaeus, Annemarie, and Mary, Serena Rogers blissfully ambles through the forest, oblivious to any concerns.

She stands about five feet four inches tall, is quite slender, and boasts some of the most exotic physical looks in all of Christville. Her face is covered in freckles, and her brilliant blue eyes sparkle with abandon. However, her most striking feature is her hair, which should be dark brown but possesses many sand-blond strands. The mass hangs loosely past her shoulder blades, free from braids or hair ties yet naturally springy and full. Her affinity for walking in the woods keeps her outside most of the day. Sledding in winter, fishing in summer, and hunting with her father in the fall are all common occurrences. She enjoys these activities very much.

However, Serena knows her outdoor activities spark the Owls' anger. Every action is contrary to the Owls' expectations for young women. However, she does not care about breaking the common mold and ignores them no matter how they view themselves. After all, what can they do outside of yelling at her?

Serena leisurely approaches the back door to her house. The structure has been waging a prolonged war with the forest beyond for control of the backyard. Her face is smeared by a shallow mask of dirt and sweat. Upon sighting the battered fence that circumnavigates her family's property, Serena activates her mental brakes. The gate creaks as she opens and shuts it. Her sneakered feet tread lightheartedly across the backyard to the screen door to the house. The screen door bangs against the metal doorframe as it closes.

At that moment, Serena sees her father, Sheldon. His height is quite average for men, but Serena finds herself consistently looking up at him to have a conversation. His hair is blond and short, blending perfectly with the orderly, well-trimmed whiskers on his chin and cheekbones. He appears young and handsome. His job as the associate pastor preoccupies him with church business. However, he always tries to spend time with his wife.

Sheldon looks toward his eldest daughter, alerted by her arrival by the screen door. "Your mother wants to see you in the parlor as soon as possible. So, you're going to want to dress in something more appropriate," he says. "She looks like a perfect storm."

"I'll get to it." Serena bolts up the stairs to her bedroom.

Her room has a bed with the covers sluggishly folded at one end, a complementing but crowded nightstand with a flashlight standing precariously on the edge, a hopelessly messy desk, and an overflowing closet. Clothes are strewn about as if they matter little to her. The walls are lined with various trophies claimed from hunting quests with her father. Their diversity might not surprise the average hunter, but others would marvel at the various critters, birds, and even four sets of deer antlers. Serena enjoys basking in the glory of her trophies, especially touching and stroking the soft furs. However, today she does not retrieve them. Instead, Serena readies herself to meet her mother.

Quickly discarding two shorter skirts and a longer dress that was stained a long time ago, she settles on a dark blue dress with gold trimmings and a worn hem. Within three of the minutes allotted to her, she sits pensively on the gatekeeping couch, awaiting her mother and the next episode of their incessant argument.

CHAPTER 4

# AN UNFORESEEN TEMPEST

Annemarie strolls into the room and sits down in the disagreeable rocking chair, which holds the status of her most favored seat. Serena notes the pseudo authoritarian air radiating off her mother.

"Let me guess. You are going to try to get me to act like a lady again, and you will design a teaching routine for that purpose that will eventually break down and end in you feeling bad." Serena opens the conversation with an apathetic speech.

"Please don't make such assumptions," Annemarie says. "People will think you're a witch."

"Sorry. I was trying to lighten my mood," Serena says. She knows she is correct and finds herself smiling.

"Furthermore, you should learn to not be quarrelsome." Annemarie sighs. "As for your predictions, they are correct." That sigh would have made Serena laugh a few years ago, but this time, she controls the childish urge. Instead, the wayfarer silently wonders if more to this conversation exists than Annemarie is letting on.

A few minutes after Annemarie's word-saturated lecture, Anaeus joins the two squabbling women. Serena notes his fleeting scowl before his usual dignified manner prevails. The straight-backed chair provides a thronelike seat for him. Serena's smile immediately dissipates. According to the Farmer's Almanac in her mind, Anaeus's sudden appearance on any occasion is synonymous with a meticulously accurate forecast of massive thunderstorms accompanied by vicious, tree-uprooting winds, double pane window–shattering hail, and a category five tornado to make survival odds less predictable.

"Now, Serena, I think you know what I'm going to say, so I will avoid as many details as possible," Anaeus states. "First, your mother and I want you to learn the morals of a good household wife, as you are becoming a beautiful sixteen-year-old girl. Here is what your new schedule will be. First, you will wake up."

"Would you take pity on my poor ears and skip the morning and school routines, please?" Serena interrupts.

"Don't interrupt me. It's hardly ladylike," Anaeus responds, mildly irritated. "As I was saying, your mother will get you up for your morning classes and chores ..."

While Anaeus continues, Serena's mind begins to wander from the informal meeting. Instead of meeting her grandfather's steadfast gaze, she subtly diverts her gaze to the forest where she spends most of her time. Nothing Anaeus says is new to Serena, yet Anaeus believes every minute detail must be repeated. Another belief to which Anaeus rigorously clings is that he must repeat every point from which an audience can reap any benefit, and Serena requires many points.

On the other side of this, Serena knows that attempting to halt Anaeus would be like trying to stop a one-hundred-car freight train moving at full tilt by parking a car in the middle of the track. The repercussions are about as bad.

Serena contemplates all the ordinary, dull home classes that every mom in Christville teaches her girls from an early age. She is no exception. For last two summers, lessons have educated her on how to cook, how to knit, and how to clean. However, since being elected worst knitter in the school paper last year. Serena remembers the picture. It displayed her holding her needles with a tangled ball of string perched between the two. She had not picked up her needles again.

Serena already feels confident concerning cleaning, maintaining a household, and doing chores around the house. She persistently claims that if she were to exchange her frequent outings in the woods for various church parties, she might be considered a lady by the mothers and grandmothers of Christville.

Suddenly, Serena's attention darts back to reality quicker than a squirrel runs up a tree.

"Serena, pay attention!" Anaeus bellows.

Caught by surprise, Serena blurts, "What? Sorry!" Her teeth dig into her lip.

Anaeus, on the other hand, growls in anger. His face clenches and turns a rousing shade of purple. His fists tightly grip the armrests of his chair.

"If my reputation wouldn't suffer for my actions, I would expel you from church!" Anaeus shouts.

Serena can only absorb the words and mentally cover her ears as the storm continues.

"You will not talk back to me! You will listen to my admonishment and obey it!" Anaeus's face is now a plethora of different colors.

When Serena fails to answer, he decides more loud words are necessary. The light shower she enjoyed three seconds earlier transforms into a huge hurricane.

"I expect an answer!" Anaeus yells with a hoarse voice and pants between each syllable.

Serena smiles at this because he has worn out. Now she plots to escape the meeting. She senses the tempest is passing. Anaeus's emotional word storm is diffusing. He rests back in the chair, winded.

"Now, if this meeting was about me getting yelled at, then your mission has been a smashing success, but I think that Grandpa is tired and should go home for his late afternoon nap," Serena says, as if this is nothing more than a suggestion.

Anaeus storms out of the room, grumbling like distant claps of thunder.

"I think you've listened to enough," Annemarie says. "We will speak of this later after dinner. However, I want you to stay here for now and talk to me. You need to get ready for school tomorrow. It is the first day. I do not think you need to be specifically told what that means? Finally, I may as well say this while Mary is in earshot. I am going to recommend that you attend the party at the church this Saturday evening."

"Yes, Mom. But, why did you say that Mary was in earshot?"

"Because Mary is behind the door eavesdropping instead of being a good girl." Annemarie turns to the closed door and raises her voice. "And getting ready for school tomorrow!"

The following moment, Serena detects a noticeable scurrying noise. Her smile chooses that moment to scamper onstage like an actor. As she shakes her head, strands of hair fall across her face. She instinctively brushes them away.

"All right," Serena grumbles, standing up, hoping to escape without listening to any more of the lecture.

Annemarie, on the other hand, is not quite finished speaking. "You look so beautiful when you smile. I think Anaeus would like you to attend the party next Saturday too."

"All right. Is that everything?" Serena studies the ceiling for cracks.

Annemarie retrieves a shred of paper from the pocket of her frilly apron. "No. I will have the final say this time," she says, holding the piece of paper.

Serena's triumphant mood is replaced by one of brooding. She takes the paper and dismisses herself from the room. She assumes it is a list of more rules that she hopes to discard.

She can't shake the unnerving feeling that this wrathful lecture will not be the last she will hear from Anaeus. He will not stop yelling at her until he lies upon his deathbed. Serena smiles and quietly snorts at the comical image. She could hear Anaeus's final words: "Serena, act like the other ladies in Christville. It will be better for you." She imagines him falling back on the pillow and his life racing from his body. Safely on the expressway to heaven, his undeniable inheritance would be bestowed.

Serena decides to detour through the kitchen. She retrieves the trash can and the list is seconds from being discarded when Mary delays its disposal by smugly exclaiming, "What paper are you throwing away this time? I hope it is not another list of expectations. You really should conform to living like everyone else in Christville. Life would be so much easier for you."

Staring at Mary in exasperation, Serena plans to return her sister's argument with an elaborate refusal. "What are you trying to say this time? I hope your vain nature is not acting up again. With all sense, you should not stick your nose in others' affairs. Life would be much easier for you."

The refusal is promptly ignored. Instead, Mary seeks to cheekily elaborate on her disregarded advice by making her voice more forceful. "You should not be so stubborn! If you don't follow Anaeus's instructions, you will face punishment."

First, Serena forces herself to smile. Then, altering the tone of her voice, she coos provocatively, "Oh, so you're so concerned over my social welfare. I would not want to turn down your offer, but"—she thrusts the scrap of paper firmly into the trash--"oops, I've done a bad thing. Sorry. I should take better care of important items."

Serena races up the stairs while an infuriated Mary struggles to yell back for her sister. Her mouth stumbles over the tripwire of her words.

"Mother!" Mary shouts irately, and Annemarie strolls into the room.

"What did you start this time?" Annemarie asks.

"I just saw Serena put your new list of rules in the trash," Mary whines.

"Serena!" Annemarie summons her daughter back downstairs.

Serena quickly reappears. Another piece of paper is clenched in her hand.

Annemarie opens the conversation. "Did you just shove my new list of rules in the trash?"

"No. They're still in my hand," Serena says, discreetly handing it to Annemarie for an inspection.

Annemarie smiles as she reads it silently:

Rules for upcoming school year:

- Limit activities with guys.
- Attend ten parties, and try to at least make one friend.
- Receive A's in all classes no matter the subject (exception: piano and ballet if on list of classes).
- Be more tolerant of disliked classes.
- Smile and have fun!

However, Mary remains unconvinced. "Wait. Let me check the trash." She frantically searches the can. Spotting the paper, she proudly whisks the crumpled paper into the air. Annemarie snatches from her and smooths out the folds to discover a blank piece of paper.

Mary stands in disbelief. She cannot utter a response. Finally, her rage overcomes her unexpected shock. She stomps from the room, leaving the pair alone in the kitchen. Serena shakes her head in astonishment, realizing the trick Annemarie is playing on her. She could have gotten away without any extra expectations other than to pass her classes in the upcoming school year. Yet, she has been tricked into giving herself a set of expectations instead.

At length, Serena breaks the silence. "I think Mary's pride is blinding her to accepting others' opinions."

Bracing her weight on Serena's shoulder, Annemarie tenderly wraps her arm around her daughter.

"Whatever the reason, Mary likes her social standing and would enjoy it better if a certain older sister was not so weird. She is sensitive toward others' reputations, and if one of her friends stumbles, it is an affront to her. Mary must learn to accept others as they are. Oh, and I just noticed, Serena, you and I are going to need to go and get you a new dress. The one you are wearing is fraying," says Annemarie.

This comment causes Serena to peer down at her dress. Sure enough, the hem is starting to come loose. She looks up at Annemarie to see if she can possibly delay the trip, but Annemarie's gaze answers her questions. There will be no delays.

"C'mon Serena. You know I put some expectations on you because I love you and do not want anything bad to happen to you," Annemarie explains. She turns to Mary, who is now sulking in the living room. "Mary, get ready for school tomorrow. Focus on yourself for a change." Then she holds her hand out to Serena.

Serena reluctantly takes her mother's hand, and the pair meander out the door and into the town beyond.

CHAPTER 5

# MISERABLE TO DESIRABLE

After eating dinner and watching a glorious sunset, Serena retires to bed. She awakes the next morning refreshed. After hastily dressing in her white T-shirt and blue overalls, she hurries downstairs and sits next to Mary at the table. Breakfast turns out to be toast with butter and jam. After lingering for a short spell, Serena grabs her backpack and meanders to the school for her first day as a high school sophomore. The weather smiles down on Christville, sunny and warm. Birds sing a farewell to summer song.

The school building is an extensive complex comprised of several varying structures. Each of these hosts a particular grade. This system is further extended with a building dedicated to each subject. In addition, the high school students use a different homeroom, which is the first class of the day. A bell's alarm summons everyone. The day starts with a prayer led by the teacher who has been selected for the week, a devotion by Anaeus himself, then announcements, and last but not least, the Pledge of Allegiance.

Upon arriving at her respective schoolhouse, Serena observes several boys scattered throughout the field like settlements in Alaska. They attempt to escape the running abilities of a pursuer. Serena resists the urge to join in the game of tag with the other high school boys. She requires herself to camouflage herself as an average lady for now.

Leisurely sitting on the soft grass, Serena retrieves her class schedule from her backpack to study it. She muses over her classes for her school year. Books and Essays 2 for first hour, *Meh.* Algebra 2 second hour. *Again meh.* American Government third hour. *I need to experience that before I pass judgment on it.* Lunch break. *Next, my favorite class of this year so far,* French fourth hour. *How many language credits are required to graduate again?* Biology fifth hour. She takes a deep anticipating breath, pauses, and looks at the next class. *Meh.* Study hall sixth hour. *That class is destined to be my favorite.*

Overall, no class appears unfriendly compared to her freshman year. Narrowly passing piano and ballet classes had resulted in some neighbors not being able to sleep because of some "talks" Serena, Annemarie, and Anaeus had at the end of the school year. Serena outspokenly despises dancing or performing in any way.

Her interest in her schedule wanes, and Serena intently stares at the exciting game of tag. Her eyes follow the players as they race around the field.

"Hey, Serena. I hear you have piano seventh hour and classic ballet for the optional eighth hour!" yells a raucous voice. It sounds suspiciously like Mary. The remark abruptly speeds Serena's attention back to reality.

Her mouth readies to return fire, but the bell rings, summoning everyone to homeroom. She moodily rises and strolls into the building. She wonders how deleterious this school year will be.

The homeroom has a common interior for any school in America. A simple wood panel floor, uncomfortable metal chairs in rows, the customary small desks in front of the chairs, and the various school supplies lining the walls. All are present for any day. Serena selects a chair in a back row. Nobody sits next to her, but she does not care. Instead, she stares ahead at the chalkboard at the front of the room.

After the prayer, Serena retrieves her schedule again. After scanning through the first six hours, her gaze settles on the two most dreaded classes: seventh hour, piano, and the optional eighth hour, ballet. *I have two arts credits from last year. I am sure only one is required to graduate. Aren't there any other electives to take? Perhaps acting or weaving or debate. I think I would like debate, but I don't want piano and ballet.* The revelation unbalances her morning, and a moody feeling settles over her like gloomy rain clouds.

Lunchtime finally arrives, and Serena sits outside because the day is warm and sunny. She reclines alone on a bench outside her next class and silently watches the walking, talking, and eating activities of lunch break before her. The peaceful solitude distracts her from her routine. Then she notices a large teenage guy named Jack Irving walking toward her.

Serena knows Jack from football after school. Jack's father is Joseph, who is better known by the title of Dr. Irving. Dr. Irving practices medicine and makes house calls any time of the day. She is also familiar with Jack's grandfather, Jonas Irving, who was an Owl and an accomplished physician as well but died a few years ago. Serena also knows Jack's mother, Mariah, is the daughter of a current Owl in Gregory Finch as well as a high school teacher at Christville school. She's heard gossip that Mariah is the most disliked teacher.

Serena can describe Jack with three words: big, tall, and fast. His kind face receives support from his bright smile and dark brown eyes. His hair is almost black and combed down on his head. He is tall and lean with long limbs, massive hands, and quick feet. The quick feet are not natural. He is described as the physical epitome for all Christville and has the courage of a lion and the leadership skills of a military sergeant. He leads the younger generation in Christville, and his greatest accomplishment could be to become an Owl if he so chooses.

Serena views Jack with a steely mixture of bleak indifference and watchful suspicion. She has watched how he leads and motivates those who disagree with his orders in football. If he were to side against her in some future conflict, Serena would undoubtedly lose. She believes this is a possibility because Gregory Finch is Mariah's father. However, in reality, The possibility of Jack allying himself with Anaeus is more probable than Anaeus wanting to play football with Jack.

Serena is also aware of Jack's three younger brothers, John, James, and Jerome. Each is a rough clone of Jack. They are often discovered following him around like a loyal bodyguard troupe after games. Serena does not often hear them speak because Jack undertakes the lion's share of their conversation. His ambition is unleashed as a football player. However, Jack's parents have made their wishes known that he should go into the youth ministry. The trio do not have any meaningful conversations with Serena, and they are not friends.

However, Serena knows that Jack's football games are an escape from the chains of normalcy for the students. The players enjoy the competition without control from the Owls. Much talent can be discovered on the field with many play styles. However, every player joyfully runs out onto the field for one reason: to have fun. Jack himself enjoys his credited positions as a quarterback, linebacker, and sometimes cornerback. Several perform many positions well, while others are recognized for one or two highly developed skills.

Serena intermittently watches the games and generally enjoys it even if she does not understand the entire strategy. However, the crashing of bodies worries her, and the risk of injury keeps her far from playing this sport.

As a result, Serena is aware of these players transforming into celebrities. Numerous contestants spend much of their time off the field avoiding the incessant crowds trailing them every day. However, Jack has risen to claim the award as the greatest icon of them all. He's called the Lion of the Gridiron, and a crowd of girls tracks him all over Christville, chatting, giggling, and relentlessly attempting to gain his attention.

To solve this "popularity crisis," as many of the participants call it, they choose certain girls to act as their friends as a way to halt the potentially seductive waves that crash upon them day after day after day. These girls are often uninterested in the sport, but are actively thrust into the world where reputations become unsecured gold that others attempt to steal. These girls are referred to as "protectors" because they keep annoying people away. In return, the player is obligated to defend the girl's honor if challenged. Overall, Serena considers them to be well-off.

In short, a protector is little less than a girlfriend, but each player and their protectors wish to rename their relationship to avoid the extra scrutiny.

"So, Jack, what brings you here?" asks Serena, opening the conversation. "Nobody ever comes here without a reason."

Jack clears his throat and pauses for a brief second before speaking. "I wanted to let you know that I want you to be my protector ... please."

Serena feels as though she has been shocked with fifty volts. She remains silent, shaking her head, until the atmosphere begins to feel uncomfortable.

Jack breaks the silence. "I'm sorry if I—"

Jack's words snap Serena out of her shock. "Sorry about that; of course I'm interested. I mean, who else would not be? I'm also sorry for interrupting you."

The bell interrupts their conversation. Students and teachers trickle away for their afternoon classes. However, Serena cannot stop asking herself a simple question: *Why me?* Yet, she would play along. Maybe she can dissuade Jack from siding with her enemies if they recruit him.. After all, Jack's offer to make her a protector is a great opportunity. He's popular, handsome, and a good guy.

Once her interminable piano lesson is thoroughly butchered, Serena races out to the field where various youths are gradually amassing. They all look lean but strong. She absentmindedly meanders through them, observing their activities. For the following minutes, the everyday discourse blandly circulates.

After school brings about its homework-filled conclusion. Jack amasses his group for a football game. A crowd of excited bystanders hurries over, not desiring to miss a second of the ensuing game. The group moves to one side of the field. Two representatives from each team march to the epicenter and host a brief meeting. Another eight individuals gather with the four players, forming a tight circle. The crowd gradually hushes. A public but mumbled conversation takes place inside the huddle. Serena cannot make out who in the center is speaking. Then she notices Jack is not present.

Finally, one of the eight shouts, "Now! I want a clean game. We will call penalties if we see them. On this quarter we have the eagle, which is tales, and the person, which is heads. Tomas, what do you choose?"

"Heads," answers Tomas.

A slight *ping* vaguely echoes from the circle.

Then the original speaker announces his verdict. "It's tails, Lawrence! Would you like to receive or defer?" he shouts.

"I want the ball!" Lawrence replies.

Serena settles into the rising competition until an anonymous hand descends upon her shoulder. She turns abruptly to see Anaeus standing behind her.

"Hi, Serena. Why aren't you going home yet? It is getting late, and you have homework to complete, I'm sure," he says.

"Because I sometimes find these games exciting."

Anaeus begins to scowl, revealing that his inquiry carries more expectations than a simple answer. Anaeus opens his mouth to speak. "Come with me now. Watching these games is unbecoming of a girl your age."

"There are other girls who watch these games," says Serena, becoming exasperated. "Why won't you convince their parents that they should not watch?"

"Because, Serena, they are not my grandchildren, and my grandchildren will be held to a higher standard than the other young men and women in Christville," Anaeus answers in his usual pompous tone.

"If I was actually held to your standard, I would never do anything fun. I would just sit around and do chores. Being a Christian is no fun," Serena grumps.

At this, Anaeus's temper commandeers the wheel of his mind. He grabs Serena's wrist and marches her away from the crowd. Once they are a safe distance away, he glowers at her and declares, "Listen here. I don't want any more objections from you. Your task is to stay silent and do what you are told. Now, you will go home and work on your homework. Is that clear?"

"Fine," Serena returns Anaeus's moody language with her own irritable retort and marches away. He watches her depart and walks away.

After traveling three blocks, Serena turns around. Not seeing Anaeus, she detours around the block and returns to the school, where the football game is still being played. She arrives during halftime.

The players from both teams mingle. Serena spots the group of elites who hold the spotlight. Lawrence chats with his quarterback, Perceval. Lawrence is recognized by his bright, reddish-brown hair, large hands, and strong frame. His blue eyes glimmer with seriousness as he and his quarterback, Perceval, whisper about the game.

While Lawrence does not have many friends, his best friend is Jack. Lawrence suffers acutely from being a nerd. Acing complicated exams in school but bombing basic social situations comprises his average track record. His family proudly shares these traits, and their creativity has resulted in numerous inventions that greatly aid life in Christville. For example, Lawrence's grandfather became famous when he constructed a functional and effective power grid using the brook north of Christville as its power source.

Finally, Lawrence and Perceval conclude their conversation. An adolescent girl takes Lawrence's arm, and the pair meander through the crowd. Serena recognizes the girl as Stephanie Trill. Her straight, reddish-brown locks fall down her back. Her bangs are restrained by a red bandanna, and her dazzling brown eyes glisten in the early fall sunshine. She appears quite pale and delicate, obviously enjoying indoor or social activities. Her glittery bright green dress shines in the daylight as she eagerly drags Lawrence's arm under the shade of the tree canopy.

With Lawrence's departure, Serena begins to observe Perceval. He is referred to as the handsome one. His dark hair covers his ears, and his face confidently wears a familiar smile. The only part of his face or body that does not attract positive attention is an aging scar that starts at his upper right cheek, curves behind his right eye, and disappears into his dark brown locks.

Serena remembers that he is young for joining Jack's football games. This is his first day in high school.

His green eyes convey ambition. He seems to not be content to labor as one of Jack's many underlings, and he never lacks ideas to eventually succeed Jack as the team's leader once Jack leaves for college. Percival is one year younger than Jack. However, Lawrence is more respected, and the other players think that Lawrence will succeed Jack. Therefore, Perceval's authority is limited to advisor and spotlight holder.

While Serena spies on Perceval, she notices another girl stroll up to him. Because Perceval and Lawrence occupy a massive chunk of popularity, a protector would be a natural person to place in their entourage. Her name is Sarah Trill, Stephanie's twin sister. She is nearly indistinguishable from her sister with her brown eyes, slim figure and reddish-brown hair that hangs in a pair of braids. However, unlike Stephanie, Sarah's face is slightly freckled and she appears to be tougher than her sister.

Sarah dresses as though she will return home via the scenic route. Serena can imagine that as soon as school concludes, Sarah will race into the forest. She is wearing a loosely fitting, white T-shirt with jean shorts. Although the pair enjoy similar activities, Sarah does not hunt and they do not talk often.

Upon sighting Perceval's protector, Serena begins to search for Jack. She turns away from the chattering crowd. She finds him conversing with two members of his team. She is familiar with their names and appearances as well. Tomas is the ordinary looking kid from an average household that owns the diner in Christville. He also works there. Arthur has a ruddy complexion.

As Serena makes her calm approach, Jack spots her and switches the conversation by saying, "I have yet to introduce you to my new protector."

"Wow. Jack finally has worked up the courage to get a protector," Tomas comments apathetically.

"Yeah, well, you probably picked the best of the lot. I should have thought of getting Serena. But I still like Alexia. She's a great girl even though she doesn't like the forest much," Arthur comments.

"She's the only girl in Christville who'll take your complaints. You know she likes you, so don't be too hard on her. You'll lose her," Tomas admonishes.

Serena watches their brief conversation unfold and dissipate. Her face portrays little emotion. Jack gently lowers his arm around her shoulder. The crowd surrounds the two teams as Lawrence, Perceval, and their protectors meander over. The reaction to Jack's news comes in the form of aloof comments ranging from groups of six to two.

"You didn't mention anything about getting a protector, Jack," Lawrence starts. His confused protector stands in front of him.

"You can't go wrong with Serena," Tomas says.

Overall, Serena feels that her admission into Jack's inner circle is respected with a measure of surprise, but nothing overtly negative is openly expressed. She spends the rest of the game excessively chatting with the other protectors. Sarah and Stephanie introduce Serena to the other protectors and welcome her. However, Alexia wants to talk to Jack about his choice. Tomas's and Josiah's protectors, Rachel Allen and Leah Taylor, appear confused.

Serena watches the rest of the game with Stephanie and Sarah. After the game concludes, the trio split up to find Jack, Lawrence, and Perceval. Serena finds Jack conversing with his brothers about how the game went. Upon spotting Serena, Jack dismisses his brothers and walks up to her. The pair stroll away from the lingering crowd of spectators and players.

Jack decides to begin a conversation.

"Can I ask you to attend the party this Saturday? I have some unfinished business I want to settle with you."

"Why don't we settle this now?" asks Serena.

"If it's OK, I would like us to be friends, and I would like to settle that soon." Jack's voice wavers in nervousness.

Serena halts suddenly. She is shocked by Jack's request. Apparently, being a protector means more than maintaining a façade of friendship to help a member of Jack's group. And so soon as well.

"I don't know, Jack. I mean, we've only been together for a day. Why?"

"Because I don't want to just act like we're friends to others. I want our relationship to be real. Then we don't need to fake anything and act like different people in public. I've seen some promising young players lose their reputation because they would not commit to their protectors or she would not fully accept him." Jack nervously quivers through his explanation.

However, Serena remains silent, thinking.

"Just think about it for now. I don't need your answer right away."

"OK, Jack."

The two depart to their respective houses.

CHAPTER 6

# THE PARTY

Despite the arranged meeting with Jack, Serena thinks of the party like an annoying, uninvited house guest who wants to stay for the day. She knows that she is supposed to be excited about the celebration, and she knows that everyone thinks she is lying. She is uninterested by these gatherings, so she avoids parties at most costs. She prefers to be out in the forest rather than at another boring church party.

Everyone attending typically brings a food dish and dresses up in suits and dresses even though many of the children do not wear formal attire. Everyone is invited, unless they recently and publicly fell out of favor with the Owls.

Serena thinks her sister, Mary, is a proud peacock with a pink puffy dress with frilly roses and curled hair with a jeweled hair band. She watches as Mary struts past her door. Mary is ready for the party and has an excited look that plays across her sister's face like a bouncing ball rebounding off every wall in the house. Mary asks for a comment about her appearance. Serena takes this as an opportunity to make a joke. Mary flies out of the room in tears, and Sheldon goes to smooth out her wrinkled feelings. Serena finds her sister's reaction quite satisfying. As a result, Mary maintains a healthy distance between herself and her older sister on the walk to the church. Sheldon is dressed as though he is preparing to preach on Sunday with a yellow tie and gray jacket

On Saturday evening, Serena walks to church. She is wearing a new sleeveless turquoise dress that drops to her ankles. It has replaced the worn-out dark blue dress Serena had worn during the last scolding with Anaeus. It does not contain hoops, unlike many of the other girls, because Serena hates hoops and extra adornments. Her hair is braided into one thick rope that cascades over her left shoulder like a gentle fountain. Overall, she considers herself a dazzling picture without too much glitter.

Outside, the church appears dark because of the sleeping sun, but the stained-glass windows cause the church to glow in the dark, radiating light to all in Christville. Light shines through the different colored glass, casting red, green, yellow, and blue hues upon the surrounding buildings, drawing residents from all over the community. The entrance to the church is lit by a pair of lanterns that dwarf the exotic lightshow outside. Majestic candles glow in their sconces on the walls. The double doors are slightly open.

Sheldon holds the door open while his family trickles in. From there, they walk into a spacious room lit by a large chandelier. The walls are white, and the floor has green carpet. A few small benches are placed underneath the small stained-glass windows in the front. On the other side, the red and rough doors to the worship center stoically guard the entrance.

Mary instantly disappears, searching for her friends, while Sheldon and Annemarie meander arm in arm to the small army of older adults that are flocking around Anaeus. Meanwhile, Serena sidles around the adults when she glimpses Jack beckoning her. Nothing appears awry, so she nonchalantly walks over and sits with him.

"I don't think the party has started yet," yells Jack over the hurly-burly of the room.

"Well, at least we can talk now," replies Serena.

"Actually, I have a better idea. Come with me," Jack bids her as he rises from the bench.

Serena follows close on his heels. He approaches an undecorated door that hides behind a gap in the church parlor's far side. He momentarily stops at where Lawrence is conversing with his protector, Stephanie Trill and a group of other young men and women. She's wearing her customary bandanna over her smooth reddish-brown locks. He snaps his fingers, and Lawrence obediently excuses himself from the conversation to silently rendezvous with the couple. Lawrence's protector nods and follows. Quickly checking to make sure that nobody is looking, Jack quietly opens the door, and the pair of couples slip through.

CHAPTER 7

# THE BELFRY

The door shuts, and the darkness envelops the quartet like an uncomfortable blanket. Making as little noise as possible, they make their way up the narrow passage. Jack half crawls, half crouches ahead while guiding his footsteps to keep the floorboards from creaking. Then, Serena senses herself ascending a flight of tight, steep stairs.

Jack scampers faster, and the floorboards begin an eerie chorus below them, shouting as though attempting to alert those downstairs of the intruders' presence. Jack stops, and Serena nearly plasters her face into his back. Holding a finger to his lips, Jack smiles. The startling creak and screaming of old metal shatters the necessary silence. The startling sound rushes into the cramped chamber. It lasts less than ten seconds, and Jack seems to vanish into the ceiling.

Serena panics for a moment until before a long beam of moonlight streams in, revealing a small ladder bolted into the wall where Jack was just crouched. The gap between the floor and the low ceiling only requires four sturdy rungs. After swiftly scaling the bottom pair of rungs, Serena gathers her physical capacities, jumps, and hauls herself up and over the edge, where she finds Jack and his big friendly grin. One prompt scan confirms their arrival in the church belfry.

The belfry is small and perched on top of the church's steeple. It is open for fresh air. A large bronze bell hangs overhead, while the ropes disappear into the eerie darkness of the abandoned floors below. A high railing lines the perimeter of the platform as well as the center gap in the floor. In between all the nighttime beauty, framed by lady midnight herself, stands a smiling Jack. A few moments later, Lawrence and Stephanie climb out of the trapdoor on the right side and immediately resume their indistinct conversation.

"Welcome to our secret hideout," Jack declares, spreading his arms wide.

"Makes sense you'd have a hideout. Are you sure you want me to know your secret?" Serena does not believe he would choose this spot over anywhere in the forest. Her secret hideaway is located there. "But couldn't you pick someplace less risky?"

"Ah, where's the fun in that?" Lawrence pauses his midnight chat to cut into Jack's tour. He flashes the pair a wry smile.

"Besides, anyone can make a lean-to or tepee in the forest. Who would suspect my hideout to be in the church's belfry?" Jack's arms absentmindedly drop to his sides.

"There is something special about this place. But nobody is allowed up here. You could get in serious trouble," Serena exclaims fearfully, her voice rising in a steady crescendo.

"No one has ever caught us here. We've been up here for years," Jack says. "We used to sneak up here during parties when we weren't being introduced to people who would pinch our cheeks and remark on how we've grown because they have dementia. The reason I wanted you to come up here was so we could get away from the public spectacle."

"It is nice to get away from the crowds, especially since nobody comes to the belfry. Why did you bring me up here?" Serena asks.

"Well, um, I wanted to show this place to you in case the parties below got too unbearable, and as I said before, I want to be friends. I mean, I thought this was a good idea," Jack replies. "Anyway, I wanted to discuss my invitation to become friends without all the commotion."

Serena is very thoughtful about Jack's offer. She keeps herself to herself and does not have friends. Nobody in Christville boasts her exact age, hobbies, and gender at the same time. Older residents criticize her, the younger generation studiously follows their example, and those with similar preferences as her shun her. Serena considers them all rather senseless. She gazes over the village below, admiring the view from the precipice. Thoughts swirl in her mind as Serena weighs her options. She is tempted by Jack's offer of friendship, but she is still not used to friendly pursuit. Finally, she turns around and faces Jack.

"I don't know what to say." Serena feels her lips quiver and her voice shakes like an earthquake rocking the mental fiber of her being. "I hate these parties too and love to get away from them."

The look on Jack's face conveys inward celebration. The quartet remains in the belfry for about an hour. They talk in whispers and tell jokes about the owls. After a long talk, they begin their tiptoed descent from the belfry. While sneaking down the old stairwell, Jack suddenly halts. They cannot hear any noise from downstairs. Lawrence and Stephanie whisper uncomfortably behind them. Serena fretfully gestures her concern about being caught.

"I'll go out first," Jack volunteers in a whisper. "So, if I'm caught, I won't get in as much trouble, and you can escape while they're preoccupied with me."

Serena does not speak. However, she nods as a sign that she understands. Jack flashes his big grin and signs to her to get back into the darkness. She retreats into the blackness. Jack advances cautiously toward the door. Every move he makes receives the utmost care. The door creaks open. Jack maneuvers himself with his back to the door. But nobody is in the fellowship room.

"Nobody's here," Jack whispers back to them.

Serena walks confidently through the door and clears all the cobwebs from her dress. Her face is adorned with a thoughtful expression. Lawrence and Stephanie follow.

"If we went into the basement together, we would be up to our ears in trouble," Serena explains. "But if we go down one at a time, people won't be nearly as suspicious. If we're challenged, we can just claim we need to go to the bathroom. Nobody will be the wiser most likely."

"Let's do this," Jack murmurs and goes first.

Lawrence marches smartly through the door, and Stephanie follows a few seconds later. However, Serena cautiously waits a few minutes before plunging into the worship sanctuary.

Right away, she notices two strong men pinning Jack's arms to the floor. Lawrence is in a similar situation. Stephanie appears distraught, covering her face with her hands. All three are undoubtedly surprised. Serena spots that one of the men has received a slight cut on his lower lip, and many chairs are being diligently hauled back into position.

She does not want to be caught gawking at the tragic scene before her, so she subtly moves around the spectacle, keeping her eyes down. She strolls to the food tables and grabs a plate. She is serving herself some of Mrs. Irving's delectable quiche when a winded-looking Anaeus walks over to Serena and barks, "Do you know anything about Jack over there?" He gestures with his arms to indicate the teen on the ground.

"No. I was in the bathroom. Besides, I don't wonder about such things. I'm a lady," Serena lies. She tries to remain calm but feels her countenance slipping.

Anaeus scowls at her, sensing his granddaughter's discomfort. "And, you're sure? Dating is not becoming of a girl like you. Are you lying to me?"

She looks straight into Anaeus's cold eyes. "No. I'm not," she calmly and evenly states, allowing her composure to relax.

"Don't talk to me like that, young lady. You should be respectful to your elders," Anaeus retorts pompously.

Serena inhales a deep breath and composes herself. "No, I am not lying to you. I do not know anything about what has happened," she reiterates in a gracious tone.

Anaeus glares at her with suspicion, but she turns and flounces away, breathing a hidden sigh of relief. Her imagination draws up what punishments Anaeus would inflict upon the trio. She guesses that Jack and Lawrence will get off easily after cleaning the party up and Stephanie will be severely scolded. She plans to apologize to them on Monday and thank them for showing her their secret.

Serena looks for a vacant table to sit alone as she wanders among the tables. However, she notices Sarah beckoning her over. Two other girls that she recognizes as Alexia and Penny. Serena always associates Alexia as being prim, proper, and pious with long, gold curls, pale skin, a gaunt face with a sharp jawline and always wearing some kind of frilly dress. This dress is turquoise checkered supported by some pale frills around the border. Serena guesses that Alexia modifies this dress. Serena always tries to avoid Alexia because she does not want to think of what Alexia would say. Alexia is also Arthur's protector.

Meanwhile, Penny ties her long, reddish-brown hair in a ponytail that is draped down her back and touches the seat of her chair. Her round face is flush and rosy. Serena is aware of her chest always appearing large no matter what she is wearing. She is wearing an airy, bright-green dress that falls to her knees. Serena can slightly make out the border of her white leggings. Serena is not sure if Penny is a protector. She is still in middle school, and all the protectors that Serena can remember are high schoolers.

Serena sits down at the table with the other three girls, picks up her fork and begins to eat. However, the other girls strike up a conversation.

"So, Serena, what do you think of Jack?" Asks Penny

"I don't know. He's a really good guy and handsome too, but he wants me to be more than his protector and to get closer to me, and it feels like we'd marry soon." Answers Serena

"Serena, Jack is the most popular kid in the school. Why would you turn him down? Are you that used to being alone?" Laughs Penny.

"Maybe I want to be left alone?" Replies Serena

"Well, it appears that the world won't" Alexia Counters, "Accept Jack. He's a good, young man. Jack chose you to be his protector. He will want to spend time with you and invest time with you."

"But Alexia everything is moving so fast and surely there are better choices than me. I am a complete rebel. I don't have friends."

"You are so used to being alone that You don't know what it's like to have others take an interest in you, and you are overwhelmed by it."

"And I had the same problem when Perceval asked me last June. I did not know what to think. He could have chosen any girl, but he chose me." Sarah exclaims because she does not want to be left out of the conversation. However, Alexia glares at Sarah and resumes encouraging Serena.

"You will do well with Jack. Just give it some time. Also, better tell your parents about what you and Jack are doing. They will want to know."

"Yes Alexia." Serena calmly refocuses on her plate and begins eating.

However, her relief is fleeting. Serena notices Mary sitting next to another guy she does not recognize straightaway. She indifferently averts her eyes, as her sister's business is not her business. She returns to the other girls sitting at the table.

"How do you suppose that Jack, Lawrence and your sister got caught?" Asks Serena

"It does not matter how they were caught. They broke the rules." Answers Alexia

"Breaking the rules or not. It was quite creative. The belfry is your secret hideout." Comments Penny

"If it is their secret hideout, how long do you think they have been sneaking up there? This is like the first time they were caught." Sarah seems to side with Serena with her question.

"You two might not like what I'm saying, but someone probably told on them." Replies Alexia.

"Don't tell anyone about this please, but I was also with them and was not caught. Why would that happen?" Questions Serena

"I don't know. Maybe they did not see you." Answers Sarah.

A shocking realization draws itself into her clouded, disturbed mind. Her gaze settles on the next table, where Mary is sitting with the other boy. Suddenly she remembers. The boy's name is Toby Bryanson. Everyone in Christville knows Toby. His size takes on the tall and lanky trend common among Christville's youth. However, his face is clear and without freckles. He has dark almond-shaped eyes and pale skin, suggesting he prefers the indoors to the outdoors. His favorite hobby includes logic puzzles and games of that sort.

However, Toby's reputation can be summed up in one word: cheater. If the puritan society were to brand one letter on his chest, it would the letter C. Everybody knows he cheats on everything and on everyone at least once. This summarizes his invisible traits and character. However, Toby has many more strengths. He does not display them often but quietly works hard for his benefit. *Could you have told on Jack? If then, why not on me as well?*

Toby's family gives him satisfactory credentials for people to assume he is a satisfactory, young man. His father, Rufus Bryanson, diligently works in the meat processing plant as a supervisor and manager whose authority can only be blocked by the legitimate owner, Oceanus. His mother is an influential person in the lady's society.

In her paranoid mind's eye, Serena can trace her sister talking among her antagonists like old friends. *Surely no good can come of this*, Serena's mind preaches repeatedly. *What in reputation ruination is Mary thinking? Or is she thinking at all?* That sentence replays in her head until she drops into bed that night with ominous opinions about Mary's new friend.

Penny is kept late after the party because her older sister had contracted some stomach problems due to the food. Now, she is walking home after obtaining permission from her elder sister to return home. She is about to push open the doors outside when a large figure darts in front of her.

"Wait, what!" Penny is startled.

"Don't be alarmed. I just need to know if Serena actually went into the belfry with those three."

"Why would you want to know that? I'm not supposed to tell anyone."

"Well, you'll be telling me now. You need not know why."

"Ok, Serena went into the belfry with Jack, Lawrence and Stephanie. Will you please let go of me!" Sarah is now quite frightened. Something trips her up and she collapses to the floor. Her panicked scream is cut shot a something being pushed into her mouth and being dragged off to one side of the room.

CHAPTER 8

# SEASONS

If all joy and happiness could be bundled into one holiday, that holiday would be Christmas for Serena, and it is approaching. The residents of Christville go out to fell and trim the small evergreen trees. The church caretakers erect the nativity on the front steps. Joyous carols are sung by assorted choirs or self-proclaimed solo artists, and playful snowball fights replace the commonplace football games that typically dominate after-school activities. The famed Christmas spirit permeates the town.

Serena participates in nearly every snowball war. She prefers this to football because it is a simpler game. She thinks many of the other protectors feel the same way. Meanwhile, her friendship with Jack has grown like the summer wildflowers. Her presence within Jack's youthful community becomes commonplace. It's soon as if Serena and Jack have been friends for a long time.

In the early afternoon of Christmas Eve, Serena lounges contentedly on her bed, thinking of what to give to Jack for Christmas. Her thoughts are interrupted when someone knocks on the door to her room. It is Annemarie.

"Jack is downstairs in the kitchen. He wants to see you," Annemarie says.

Serena cheerfully hurries downstairs. She is dressed in her

usual overalls and T-shirt and has a severe case of bedhead. Johnny Appleseed cares about his personal appearance more than her. Everyone in Christville knows about Serena's abnormal dress code. She speeds into the kitchen and discovers Jack seated at the kitchen table. Annemarie, who has followed her, silently exits the room.

"Hi. I wasn't expecting you," Serena exclaims.

"I came to ask you what you wanted for Christmas," Jack replies.

Serena thinks only for the briefest moment before answering. "To go swimming this summer! That would be my biggest wish," Serena gushes.

"Now, that is quite a request," Jack says, flashing his big grin.

"I'm sure you will work it out," Serena says. "I was going to ask you what you wanted for Christmas. I know you loved the jerky from your birthday two months ago."

"Oh, yeah. That was really good. Better get two cases this time." Jack's grin widens at the thought. Then he rises, retrieves his coat from the hanger, and marches out into the frozen world.

Before Jack can fully vacate the yard, Annemarie discreetly halts him and says, "Don't worry about Serena's request. I will take care of it."

Meanwhile, Serena retreats to her room and shuts the door behind her. In the privacy of her bedroom, she surveys her available assets. Her excitement bubbles over with each coin and bill she counts. Upon a meticulous inspection of her savings, she determines she has enough money to purchase the present and then some.

CHAPTER 9

# THINGS EXPECTED AND UNEXPECTED

Later that evening, every house in Christville seems to burst with excitement as families prepare for the most wonderful time of the year. The Rogers are no exception to the infectious happiness. Mary flies about the house, getting ready for the Christmas party at the church. Every other event at the church significantly pales in comparison. All families in Christville consistently come, regardless of their reputation.

On this occasion, Serena selects an airy red dress with a white lining. The dress is solid red on top and becomes more translucent around her arms and around the white skirt's border. However, she is also considering another dark-green dress with a knee-length skirt and a white lace pattern on the front. Since Serena can't decide on which dress to wear, she walks to her mirror to arrange her hair for the Christmas party. Serena is finishing her thick braid to adorn her shoulder when Mary disturbs the tranquility of her room. Mary is wearing a red dress detailed by an intricate, white lace pattern on the front, with hoops that take up half the room. Her hair is bedecked with a glittering silver tiara. Mary initiates the tense conversation.

"Unlike you, I was able to nab someone's affections. I have been trying to tell you that for a while now," Mary declares in a querulous tone.

Serena raises her head slowly. Noticing Mary in the mirror's reflection, Serena scowls. In that moment, she feels like the gloves have been thrown off. She is not interested in a peaceful Christmas conversation.

"Charm is deceitful, and beauty is vain but ...,"[2] Serena says without turning her face from the mirror, but she does not watch Mary. Serena thinks of how to make Mary feel insulted. "Besides, you look like a flower in full bloom."

"Excuse me, but you're the one with the laxer dress code. What right do you have to judge me? And, since we're talking in Bible verses, I'll tell you to take the log out of your own eye before taking the splinters out of your brother's eye, or in this case, sister's. Tee-hee-hee,"[3] Mary retorts angrily.

"Well, I'm still not the one who looks like a ghost with a head full of flowers at every party," Serena growls in reply. She feels her own temper rising while returning her sibling's biblical broadside.

"Yeah, but you should be more concerned about your company. Those boys could mean trouble. Also, have you forgotten that whoever walks with the wise grows wiser, but a companion of fools suffers harm?" Serena feels Mary's disdain as she piles on the sass on by the truckload.

"How do you know Jack is a fool? All he has done is treat *me* with respect. Something that does not happen *here* very often," Serena demands, hoping to terminate the argument.

When Mary fails to answer, Serena commences the complete annihilation of Mary's foray with one final verbal blow.

"Well, it seems like I nabbed a crowd and you only have one,"

---

[2] Proverbs 31:30.
[3] Matthew 7:3–5.

Serena exclaims while fighting the urge to forcefully evict the loathsome little leech from the room.

Mary does not wait for Serena's inevitable order and flounces from the room with a pretentious air and her head held high. Serena grimly returns to her reflection. After several minutes of reconsideration, Serena decides to wear her green dress. She cannot stand the idea of looking like Mary.

Upon entering the party, a short while later, Serena immediately escapes her parents' eyes to converse with her friends. If the earlier blaring events had been a radio broadcast, the front room now sounded like a concert at a huge stadium. After many words and laughs, Anaeus forcefully opens the large red doors to the sanctuary, and everybody methodically files in. The intense noise follows the crowd like annoying mosquitos tracking each person.

The sanctuary has the highest seating capacity in all Christville, extending many yards in two directions. Even though there are only four rows of pews split by five aisles, each ornately carved pew has a substantial reach. The floor is covered in a stonelike tile. In front of the sanctuary, the choir loft boasts three short pew-like rows. Two wooden boxy structures with picturesque craftsmanship proudly occupy both sides of the stage. They stand like a pair of stoic bodyguards.

The comparatively quaint podium from which messages are preached to the congregation retains a dignity that does not require elegant carvings or detailed depictions. Its frontal placement bestows its status, and it remains in its position, though it can be an obstruction during certain events, including this one. Most residents do not notice, as everyone's eyes are trained in wonder on the glorious tree. It is very tall with thousands of precious crystal ornaments. Many long glowing candles create a rustic atmosphere and fill the room with the smell of oily wax. Wreaths adorn each stained-glass window like little crowns; they are also lit by their own personal candles. In front of the podium, the decorative altar blesses the crowd with its red, green, and white decorations.

Serena and her family immediately step into the worship center of and sit down. First, Annemarie files into the pew, followed by Mary and Serena. Sheldon sits on the edge of the pew so he can leave quickly.

The gifts are scheduled to be distributed in five minutes, and the bottom of the tree is already crammed with presents. The lofty fake evergreen in the center of the stage nearly touches the ceiling. The Owls painstakingly sort the gifts according to their destinations. Serena observes them hustling away like a busy nest of five ants.

After the gifts are sorted, Gregory clears his throat loudly to demand everyone's attention, and the room falls silent. Next, Anaeus narrates the Christmas story from the Bible while the audience respectfully listens. Then a representative from each family retrieves the presents for his family. Meanwhile, the chatting, yelling, and celebrating residents briskly reignite their noisy conversations. Normally, the fathers within each household represent their families. Serena wants to accompany her father to help him with the numerous gifts from their many friends. Sheldon returns carrying a massive armload of presents and distributes them to his wife and girls.

Serena looks over at her sister as Mary receives a new set of fancy hair ties. Her old set has been fading. Mary's overjoyed smile conveys her reaction to everyone.

Serena collects few gifts from others outside her family except hilarious cards, which she appreciates. She does not give people very many ideas for gifts, so people never know what to give her. However, Serena acquires new ammunition and cleaning supplies for the twenty-two she received for her birthday two years ago. One Christmas, she received a pocketknife, and it is one of the few items of which she jealousy keeps track. The blade is three inches long, and the hilt has a fancy wood pattern carved into it. Serena maintains the blade so it is razor sharp and keeps it with her on most occasions.

However, this Christmas Serena is handed a flat package, but she is not sure who gave it to her. She raises her eyes to the pews ahead of her, peering at each self-absorbed and celebrating family.

She knows the Owls are watching, especially her grandfather, and steels her nerves. She must be cautious. Wanting to avoid another angry altercation, she refrains from opening the package and decides instead to enjoy it later. However, she takes the wrapping off so she does not appear ungrateful.

Just before she extracts her present, she slightly starts and scans the entire gathering. She notices Anaeus passing their pew, shaking hands, laughing, and briefly congratulating the families he passes. Unlike during their past encounters, he seems happy and content. However, Serena decides to stay alert, for Anaeus can swing his mood from cheerful to downright irate in about three seconds.

"Well, Serena, what did you get for Christmas this year?" Anaeus asks in a jovial manner.

"I would tell you, but I don't think you'd like it," Serena replies.

Anaeus's face begins to darken, but Sheldon speaks up. "Anaeus, this is Christmas."

Anaeus relaxes his face and marches on, shaking people's hands as he goes. Watching him depart leads Serena into the depths of her mind. *When have I last been scolded by Anaeus?*

It was when Anaeus accused her of lying to him. This leads her to wonder why it had been so long.

Myriad responses rush to her mind, attempting to explain the phenomenon. Maybe her parents had intervened to stop Anaeus, or perhaps he hadn't been in the correct mood.

*I need advice, but I don't want my parents to know. I feel that they could bungle the entire situation*, Serena concludes in the privacy of her own thoughts.

Meanwhile, the opening of presents is followed by a large potluck supper with so many different foods. She walks up to Jack after he serves himself a large platter of meatballs on top of mashed potatoes and corn. Before she can properly address him, she spots Mariah, Jack's mom, staring at her angrily.

"Jack, what's wrong with your mom?" Serena whispers.

""She does not approve of our relationship. She has talked to me about it, and I can see why she doesn't like you, but I still want you and that's not changing."

The pair find a table occupied by a pair of Jack's closest friends, who are chatting with their protectors. Lawrence and Stephanie admire the wooden sword Lawrence made for her, while Perceval and Sarah talk around their own plates of food.

"Still, something's not right. I could feel it while everyone was opening presents," Serena whispered urgently.

"What would be wrong? Did the Owls yell at you again?" Jack asks.

"It's the lack of yelling I'm concerned about. If the Owls see something they don't like, they confront that person head-on, but what I'm seeing are little less than disapproving looks from them. This is not their style."

"I understand," Jack replies casually. "Just be careful. If the Owls strike, it can be for anything, and when they do, you can always count on me to help."

"It would be more helpful if I knew how the Owls intend to act. That would make preparing for their attempt easier." Serena feels as though one thousand pairs of eyes have fixed themselves upon her.

Jack remains silent but nods. His gaze travels across the great room. He excuses himself and joins some of his friends.

Serena returns to her listless ponderings. Her eyes scan every individual in the room. She spots Mariah, Jack's mother, again. Their gazes meet. Mariah's eyes narrow into an irate grimace. Serena returns her stare with a steady gaze. Mariah glares at her. She appears to be plotting, but she says nothing. Maybe she does not want to humiliate herself at the Christmas Eve church party. Finally, both parties' drop eye contact and continue their respective festivities.

CHAPTER 10

# THE CONFLICT BEGINS

While the people of Christville assemble to eat the annual the Christmas Eve dinner, Anaeus summons the other Owls. Once they are effectively isolated in a side room, he speaks up.

"You all have heard of the exploits of my rebellious granddaughter Serena. She must be halted in her unrighteous behavior. She sets a crude example for the younger generations," Anaeus declares.

At this, the hall falls silent. Then another voice speaks up. This voice belongs to Oceanus. "Perhaps we should consider that she is friendless among the ladies her age. No one wants anything to do with her. Recall your daughter, Anaeus, and how her loneliness urged her away from the other ladies and into sinful behavior."

"Don't remind me of my daughter! I remember well!" Anaeus becomes annoyed. "But do you recall that I opposed her behavior until she quit? Serena must represent a good example for the other young girls soon to be her age."

"Anaeus, you know that Serena would reply that Christville's mothers provide adequate examples for good behavior. She is more than capable of using our own practices against us," Oceanus replies. "You should better evaluate your arguments. Especially if we want to respond to her. If you recall correctly, Serena has wit as the swamp oak has leaves."

"I admit that you have a good point," says Anaeus, who is hoping to end the deriving debate. It is wasting his time. Taking a deep breath, he continues, "I wholeheartedly believe we must squash this threat before it becomes a crisis. If you learn one thing from reading the Bible, it's that the next generation is fickle and bad. Serena is a bad example. She'll lead the entire population down into sin and corrupt our community."

This is a common lesson to explain how current youths destroy the moral codes upon which Christville is firmly grounded. Anaeus smiles inwardly. His fellow colleagues might be smart, but they would never contradict the Bible.

Gregory shatters the triumphant silence. "I say this neither against the Scriptures nor your intellect, Anaeus, but I have a problem believing that Serena is a threat. She is an isolated case, you have not offered any specific sin, and she has not led the next generation into sin. She has no followers. Thus, we do not need to do anything against Serena, your granddaughter. Mind you, Anaeus ..." Gregory pauses and motions to the door. "If you asked any child in that room, they would tell you that they would refuse to accept Serena and her anarchist ways. For these reasons, I must protest your proposal."

These remarks surprise Anaeus, and his frustration mounts. The Owls have put up a more stubborn defense than he anticipated and seem reluctant to act. His thoughts regroup and press forward in a renewed offensive. He triumphantly plays his last card, which happens to be an ace.

"But you are blind to her activities like we were blind to her mother's. The Bible clearly states that bad company corrupts good morals, and Serena has gained the acceptance of Jack and his group. She will influence them, and we stand to lose a sizable portion of our young men. For your renowned zeal, you have grown lax in responding to bad behavior."

"Yes, Anaeus, but what has she actually done?" Oceanus asked.

"We can always make something up," Josephus said in a gruff tone.

Anaeus looks up. He feels that he is close to achieving his goal.

"But we can't just make up a bunch of crimes! We are not liars! Even non-Christians believe that is wrong. How much more will the Bible say against us if we accuse Serena falsely?" Oceanus argues.

"She is not conforming to the authorities of Christville. That is a crime in the Bible's eyes," Josephus says, attempting to quell Oceanus's argument.

Titus raises his hand for silence, and Oceanus and Josephus comply. Titus says, "I cannot condone exiling a member of this town on false claims, but I will make you a deal, Anaeus. If you have a specific sin she has committed, you will go to Serena and ask her to repent of her actions. If she repents, you will drop your grudge against her and apologize to her for being harsh on her, but if she refuses ..." Titus sighs as if he is making this decision against his better judgement. "We will exile her."

"I agree," Anaeus says.

"We agree!" unanimously declare the Owls.

Titus adjourns the private meeting, and Anaeus rejoins the boisterous crowd in the main room. He has convinced the jury before the trial starts. He smiles maliciously and orders himself to wait for the right opportunity. He knows the jury has already decided the verdict he wants.

Yet he feels these deeds may provoke a war and antagonize more powerful adversaries. Power sleeps until specific events transpire. However, that thought is fleeting and disappears like mist to Anaeus. To imagine that someone or something could possibly defeat his moral control over the community seems laughable. If a conflict is required, Anaeus will fight to defend the community even if one must be removed from it.

He will fight to ensure that his past does not repeat itself. Seventeen years ago, in early August, a messenger arrived at his house. The messenger told him that Sheldon had just prevented Annemarie from killing herself. Before this, Annemarie had been a good girl in his mind, but he should have paid closer attention. In the aftermath of that, he learned a lot of what his daughter was secretly doing. Anaeus was forced to watch as his near perfect picture of Annemarie burst into flames and fall at his feet in ashes. The memory almost brings him to tears.

Annemarie was going to have a baby, but she would not say who the father of her child was. However, Sheldon was still there and he loved Annemarie despite everything she had done. It didn't matter to him. His daughter was not worthy to marry anyone, yet Sheldon had asked her. They were married, and Serena was born not long after. Annemarie became a Christian because of Sheldon, and she remains faithful to him.

Anaeus wanted to correct his mistakes he made with Annemarie, but as Serena grew, all he could see was Annemarie's rebellion being repeated. He wanted to bring her back, but Serena was stubborn and unrepentant. Anaeus has never admitted this to Serena, but he fears she is falling down the same rebellious path as her mother. *Now, it is time. Serena shall be punished for her rebellion. Then Serena will know to never repeat those mistakes.*

"Yes," Anaeus says under his breath. "Let the incursion begin."

"Hey, Anaeus!" A voice jolts Anaeus out of his imagination and back to reality. He glances around and finds Toby staring at him.

"Oh, Toby, what trouble are you getting yourself into?"

"The real question should be what trouble are you getting into? I heard you and the Owls plotting something, and I want to know."

Anaeus blanches. He hopes Toby does not notice his blush. He does not want to divulge information about exiling his granddaughter, but Toby has forced his hand. *Oh well. I would have had to tell someone about my intentions anyway.* He turns to answer Toby, who is waiting expectedly.

"If you want to know, I have some grievances against my granddaughter Serena. And you came at the right time because I need someone to bring the charges against her. I want to appear innocent in this matter," Anaeus rumbles like an idle car.

Toby's catlike eyes sparkle as he remarks, "Oh, now that is something, Anaeus. It is truly a scheme that easily beats anything I have ever done. And what do you think if I told someone about your little scheme and ruined your perfect reputation? That might be enough payback for all those visits to your office over the school years. Maybe Serena might be satisfied, what with all those reprimands you've given her."

Toby rants about how he could get Anaeus into trouble. However, Anaeus smugly retorts, "Toby, you've forgotten who you're talking to. Need I remind you of your reputation. Nobody's going to believe a liar like you."

Anaeus notices Toby blush and his eyes go wide. He can yell Anaeus's misdeeds to every resident in Christville, but few will believe him because he is a cheat and Anaeus knows this.

Anaeus wastes no time. "You will bring charges against Serena. I'll leave it up to you what you say, but you won't tell anyone. Do I need to mention possible consequences?"

Toby clenches his fists and angrily grimaces at Anaeus, but Anaeus says nothing. Toby stomps away, grumbling to himself, leaving Anaeus alone with his thoughts again.

"Yes," Anaeus says under his breath. "Let this incursion begin."

## CHAPTER 11

# A WARNING FOR THE WAYFARER

As the days steadily warm and drive winter away from Christville, Serena recommences her wanderings in the woods. During winter, she was comfortable in school. She could talk with her new `friends and play in snowball fights. But with the warming days, Serena is bored of school. She longs for the forest and impatiently counts down the days until summer vacation.

As the weather becomes milder in late May and early June, Serena knows the boys are testing the water in the swimming holes. She does not want an ice-cold plunge and a scampering evacuation from the freezing grip of the water, so she waits to swim. To pass the time, she joins Jack's group in the woods to hike or play simple forest games like capture the flag and tag. They also plan a weekend camping trip.

The day arrives when the swimming hole is declared suitable. One glorious Saturday afternoon in mid-June, Jack's group gathers for a relaxing stroll in the forest. Every protector is invited, and most decide to attend, unlike previous excursions. After meandering through the glen, chatting in the sunny weather, everyone decides on a rousing game of tag. They play until Arthur, who mysteriously disappeared a half hour ago, is observed sprinting toward the game. His legs are soaked, but he does not appear uncomfortable. Once he catches his breath, he surrenders his newly acquired information.

"I think the swimming hole is warm enough," Arthur says, gasping.

Bedlam reigns. Some members decide they should refrain from swimming because Serena and the other protectors don't have swimsuits. Serena, Stephanie, and the rest of the protectors extricate themselves from the arguing mass that comprises Jack's group. Some of the less forest-inclined wander back toward town. Serena, Stephanie, and a handful of others who enjoy the glen and its wonders subtly form a human fence around the squabbling group. Finally, Jack's shout rises above the hubbub to silence his group like Jesus calming the roaring waves on the Sea of Galilee.

"Everybody quiet!" bellows Jack.

The sudden stillness that conquers the clearing is in clear contrast to the arguing din. For about half a minute, nobody speaks or moves. All eyes focus on Jack's large demeanor. Serena thinks she overhears the fluttering of a bird's wings in flight. After they have all recovered from the shock, Jack clears his throat and gives his decision.

"Everyone who wants to go swimming, go back home and get your swimsuits. We will meet back here in about a half hour. I will go and get an adult chaperone in case any of our protectors join us."

Everyone nods their allegiance and scatters to their various households. Serena begins to return to her abode. Jack strolls behind her at a limited distance. Serena feels puzzled by Jack following her out of the forest because his house is in a different neighborhood. After some time, Serena stops, faces Jack and asks, "Why are you following me? Is there anything you want to tell me?"

"Your wish is granted. You can go swimming now." Explains Jack.

Serena smiles back. She remembers asking Jack for the ability to go swimming last Christmas. However, now that she has it, Serena realizes that her newfound freedom appears quite dangerous.

"I. don't know what to say. Thank you, Jack. I shouldn't turn your offer down." Serena speaks softly feeling unsure about her words.

Jack approaches Serena and takes her hands into his and says, "This is what friends do for each other." Serena bows her head then Jack relinquishes Serena's hands. Serena hurries down the path, leaving Jack behind. He gradually stops and then, with a contented sigh, turns into the forest walking in the direction of his house.

Meanwhile, Serena swiftly approaches her backyard. At first, Serena feels perturbed by Jack's admission. It is replaced by an invigoratingly, calm feeling as she slips inside. As she climbs the stairs, a great *thump* disrupts her ascent. It came from the direction of Mary's bedroom, but Mary does not emerge. After a long hesitation, Serena begins to climb once again. But a familiar voice catches her by surprise.

"Ah, Serena, I was looking for you. We need to talk about your grades," Anaeus says.

Serena turns around and descends the stairs, feeling puzzled and frustrated by her grandfather's statement. Why should he care about her grades?

Anaeus continues, "Your grades are good, but there is that one C in piano that I want to address."

"What's so bad about my C in piano? I'm not talented, and I don't want to impress people by being a musician. I don't even like piano." She turns to leave.

"No, come back here, Serena. You are talented at piano but only if you practice at it. Roger girls should always try their best, and you are clearly not," Anaeus says in a pompous tone.

Serena stands at the foot of the stairs, but her concentration begins to fade. She wants to go up to her room, retrieve her swimsuit, and go swimming. Anaeus's lecture about her future, talent, and spiritual beauty does not interest her at all. She turns to climb the stairs a second time.

"I'm sorry. I have to go. I have something in my room I want to take care of, *privately.*" She rushes off upstairs toward her room before Anaeus can interrupt her.

Anaeus is left behind in the kitchen. He growls in frustration and reaches for a sheet of paper and a pen. After writing a quick note for Serena, he walks away to present his findings to his colleagues.

After sharing the new information, Anaeus withdraws to his office in the basement of the church. It is a simple room with stiff green carpet, whitewashed walls, and a plain ceiling. Bulletin boards and shelves line the walls, bedecked with important information concerning the church or historic photographs. A large desk sits in the middle of the room with a filing cabinet beside it. Normally, papers cover the desk's surface. However, Anaeus has organized his office for this occasion. After scanning the room, Anaeus leaves for Sheldon's office down the hall. He knocks on the door.

"Come in."

Anaeus opens the door, steps inside Sheldon's office, and shuts it behind him. Sheldon is studying his Bible for references for a later sermon. However, he is wasting time, as he is helping at the party that will take place this evening. Papers are scattered across his desk.

"Ah, Anaeus, what can I do for you?"

"I don't want to be the bearer of bad news, but my colleagues and I have decided to exile your daughter, Serena. She is rebellious and refuses to conform to this town's expectations for young women her age."

"You mean *your* expectations, Anaeus, and you want to exile my daughter. So, the C in piano was offensive enough?" Sheldon says with a noticeable heated edge in his voice.

Anaeus ignores Sheldon's verbal jab. "I know that you care for Serena, your daughter. However, you won't do anything, because if you do ... I will tell your congregation the truth about her. I think you can imagine what might happen if I told others about your wife's past," Anaeus threatens.

Sheldon laughs. Anaeus draws back.

"Anaeus. Everyone already knows. Go ahead and remind them. Again. If it helps, I'll do it."

"Are you serious, Sheldon? You are right! Everyone knows that Annemarie was expecting Serena. Then you spouted out lies like a fountain, telling everyone in Christville that you were the father. I see through your lies. You can't hide the truth from me this time."

"Anaeus, if my lies are so offensive, you should have disciplined me a long time ago. Frankly, why don't you discipline me now? I did what any good Christian should have done for your daughter and your granddaughter. You, however, show no Christian compassion."

"You have two choices. Do nothing and you will get your wish. *But* if you try to interfere … you will never be an Owl!" Anaeus allows his voice to trail off.

Neither Anaeus nor Sheldon speak for a little while.

"I understand. And I will never want to be an Owl."

"Good," Anaeus says. He vacates the office and slams the door behind him.

Meanwhile, Serena arrives at her room. She darts inside and locks the door. She painstakingly coaxes the flat package she received at the Christmas Eve party out from under her cluttered bed. She opens it, revealing a regular red tankini with white fastenings on the back.

Before trying it on, Serena places her ear to the door to make sure nobody is coming. Hastily, not trusting her sister's meddlesome nature, she swaps her regular outfit for the swimsuit. She admires herself in the full-sized mirror next to her wardrobe. She immediately likes it.

Serena quickly puts on her grass-stained T-shirt followed by her overalls and strides toward the door. She is rushing out of the house when Mary hurries toward her. A card-sized paper is tucked between her left thumb and pointer finger.

"Looks like the Owls are calling on you to stop your nonsense with the young men of Christville. They say that you are becoming a bad influence," Mary declares. Triumph sparkles in her eyes as if a magic fish has materialized in her hands. Frustrated, Serena drags herself to face Mary's new threat.

"Ok." Serena takes the note from Mary but does not look it. She mentally chastises herself; she should have known this was coming.

She attempts to brush past Mary, but Mary has not finished and pursues her.

"It sounds serious, and if you don't respond, it could go very poorly."

Serena stops and looks back at her sister. "What about this warning?" she asks, attempting to hide a quizzical look on her face. She casually sits down at the kitchen table.

Mary claims a seat, and Serena motions for her to reiterate the warning.

"Yesterday, Anaeus and Titus approached me at church. They demanded I deliver a message to you since Anaeus wasn't able to talk with you without getting angry. I could relay his message word for word, but in short, he requires you to attend a party with me. If you don't, or if you talk with the boys or if he thinks your dress is not elegant enough, he will denounce you. That's all." Mary attempts to conceal her emotions. "In addition, he gave me this paper."

Serena leans back in her chair thoughtfully, clutching the paper in front of her face. Her mouth hangs open in contemplation. As much of a pain as Mary could be, Serena decides not to displease her sister. She deduces that the note originated from Anaeus. She recognizes her grandfather's flowery penmanship, so she believes Mary's story.

"Very well, but I need to think about this with Mom." Serena makes her decision final and marches out the door without another word.

Serena hears the door close behind her. She spots Annemarie finishing her work in the garden. She wears a straw hat with a wide, straight rim and is holding a basket filled with the summer harvest.

"Mom, can you come over to the swimming holes with me?" Serena asks.

"Sure, Serena. I just need to set this basket in the kitchen."

Annemarie vanishes inside the house and reappears ready for an excursion in the forest. They depart into the forest and walk down the path toward the swimming hole. As Serena's mind races, she tries to think of a plan. She knows swimming with the boys is not acceptable according to the Owls, but with her mother's company, Serena is confident she will be safe.

As they approach the swimming holes, she notes their location in the clearing near the river to the northeast, which supplies them with water. The ground is somewhat unstable, so the trees in the area are quite limited. However, people can still walk there without much trouble. Many of Jack's group have been drawn to the largest of the swimming holes in the center of the clearing. The main swimming hole is surrounded by high banks. A person must jump to enter and awkwardly scramble over the stony bank to exit. The main swimming hole has two ends, one shallow and the other incredibly deep. At the highest point of the bank, an old tree hunches over the deepest part of the pool. A long rope dangles from one branch that extends over the water.

Leaping off the bluff and into the deepest depths is the most common activity there. However, endeavoring to swing out as far as possible should be avoided. This unspoken rule is enacted when a person sustains a severe injury when he or she unexpectedly rams his or her head into the shallow end. Perceval learned that lesson the hard way and paid for that with a lecture as well as a visible wound on his face.

Serena and her mother reach the large swimming hole. She notices the large crowd that is already there. They look ready for a swim. She does not see Jack. Then Jack, Perceval, and Perceval's mother show up.

Upon reaching the clearing, Jack shouts to the rest of the group, "What are you waiting for! Go swimming!"

Most of Jack's group rush at the main swimming hole, leaving their shirts and towels somewhere dry. The air is filled with the sound of shouting and splashing. At first, Serena goes to the main swimming hole with many of the others, but then decides that the main swimming hole is too crowded. She exits the main swimming area and jumps into a more secluded, shallow hole where Jack and Perceval are conversing.

"What happened while we were gone?" Perceval asks her.

Serena replies, "Anaeus wrote me a note that I have to attend the upcoming party today, and he doesn't want me to speak with you, Jack. I mean, what does Anaeus plan for me to do at the party? Stand around like a fashion queen? This is the reason why I don't attend parties. But he threatened to exile me if I don't, so ..."

Jack and Perceval react to Serena's warning with silence. By law, in Christville anybody can shun people, but that power is seldom used. However, the threat of it sends a lightning bolt of fright down upon the bravest of men. To be denounced means to risk being exiled from Christville if convicted. There is no lasting settlement for miles. Residents simply lead the condemned person past the river and leave them for a period of time. The Owls extend their sentence if someone sees that person on the other side of the river. Serena feels the seriousness of the situation and remains silent.

For a while no one speaks. Then Jack orders somberly, "According to me, there is a loophole in this warning. See, it says that you have to attend the party, but it doesn't say anything about your power to swim today."

As the perfect day for swimming continues, the trio silently sit in the comfortable water. They focus on getting Serena out of the upcoming social entanglement.

Finally, Serena says, "Listen. I know none of you will overly like this, but I think I'll get denounced even if I attend the party tonight, wear my best, and don't talk with you."

"How could you know that?" Perceval asks. "Are you a witch?"

Serena intentionally disregards him and earnestly seeks to elaborate. "You see, his warning states that if I don't dress elegantly, then I will be denounced. But that part of his ominous warning is vague for some unknown purpose. This offers them an unclear reason to denounce me even if that reason is not valid. And the fact that they've always seen me as a threat makes their plan ever more likely to succeed. I say I will get denounced anyway, so I'll try defending myself at the hearing, which always takes place on Sunday afternoon. That won't be much time to prepare myself, but I could likely win."

"If anyone can win a logical argument, you can. Oh, and by the way, because of this warning, maybe I should not attend the party," Jack says.

"Hey, the main swimming hole is starting to clear up. I think we can sneak in there undetected," Perceval says, looking over at the main swimming hole.

So, Perceval and Jack scramble out of their swimming hole. Jack takes Serena's hand to help her out, and the trio leave to have some fun on the rope swing.

## CHAPTER 12

# SECRETS NOT WORTH KNOWING

Serena hurries back home to get ready for the party. She chooses her sleeveless turquoise dress. She has just changed from her usual garb and into her dress when Mary saunters into the room. Mary wears a pink dress with puffy sleeves with her usual massive hoops underneath.

In her peripheral vision, Serena frantically notices her swimsuit lying on the floor in a heap on top of her T-shirt and overalls. She attempts to subtly shift the incriminating evidence under her bed. However, Mary notices and retrieves the swimsuit. At this point, Serena prepares for the usual confrontation.

"Hmm, what's this? It doesn't look like a dress," exclaims Mary, her voice slimier than slugs.

"It's none of your business." Serena casually turns towards the mirror and acts as though she is trying to style her hair. She hopes Mary will not encroach further.

"In fact, I think I have heard of these things," says Mary, smiling sinisterly. "My friend Toby tells me that these things are called swimsuits. You haven't been naughty and gone swimming with your crowd now, right?" she teases and holds the swimsuit aloft.

Serena darts toward Mary's hair and seizes her hairpin. The brown mass unfurls and flops into Mary's face. She screams with surprise while desperately swatting her hair into a new position. Serena capitalizes upon the moment to recapture her swimsuit. Once Mary sweeps her hair away from her shocked face, Serena stands, holding her recollected swimsuit in one hand and the stolen hairpin in the other. Controlled fury emanates from both of their expressions like steam from a boiling kettle.

"You won't be telling anyone, or I'll say that you've been disturbing me when you knew I'd be taking a bath. I might still get into trouble for harboring a possibly sinful relic, but you would be in even deeper trouble for disturbing my privacy."

A multitude of emotions cross Mary's face, from disbelief to surprise to uncontainable horror. Leaving Serena alone with the hairpin in her hand, Mary fearfully flounces out of the room. Before the family commences their stroll to the church, Serena secretly puts the hairpin on Mary's desk.

Serena feels that the party is like an oversized dull and boring sandwich with extra bland sauce on the side. She feels like no one at the party cares, and she, likewise, does not care about them. She feels the icy glares from the other girls at the table like bills in the mailbox, and the conversation would have miserably failed to gain the interest of a sleeping toad. As a result, she sits alone with her plate of mashed potatoes with thick gravy, a piece of corn bread, and a bowl of fruit. She is thankful for Jack's helpful intentions to remain home, but now she misses him.

Presently, she spots the Owls and her sister, Mary, entering a side chamber. She surreptitiously swipes an empty cup from the stand and follows them. The Owls carefully shut the door. Serena sneaks up to the door, softly places her glass cup to its surface, and listens to the conversation inside.

"Everything is ready. All we require is to get someone to file the denouncement and she's as good as guilty," reports one voice.

The Owls have very loud voices.

"May I examine the charges again so I may know them?" demands a feminine voice.

"What? Why? Why you, Mary?"

Questions flood Serena's mind.

"We are bringing Serena up on charges of conspiracy to commit mischief and subverting authority, and thanks to your report, Mary, we will be adding harboring sinful relics with malice," answers another voice that definitely does not belong to Anaeus. "Plus, I know exactly who will file these charges. Or he'll fail every one of his classes for cheating. His friend will make a second witness, for the Bible says two eyewitnesses consistently make a fact."

Serena jumps away from the door as if it has suddenly transformed into a snake. The glass falls to the floor but doesn't break. Snatching her cup, Serena nervously fills it with water and calmly steps back to her seat. She scrambles to regain a fragmented resemblance of composure, and she spies on the door for the prolonged period. Serena wants to be certain that Anaeus, Titus, and the other Owls do not suspect her eavesdropping.

When the Owls emerge, they act as if nothing outside of the ordinary has taken place. Meanwhile, Serena stealthily abandons the party on the excuse that she has contracted a sharp headache. Once those inside the church cannot observe her movements, she plots a direct course for Jack's house.

The weather is dry, warm, and comfortable, making for a luxurious trip through the dark streets. Streetlamps provide the only light for her as she strides along the empty roads. Serena arrives at Jack's house and gives an uneasy knock at the front door. When Jack answers, Serena sighs in relief.

"I just found out. The Owls are going to denounce me," she explains.

"Why? What charges do they have? Did the party not go well?"

Serena knows she needs to warn Jack. She realizes how much she wishes her differences were not so threatening to the Owls. She knows now that most people like Jack do not have to worry about being rejected.

"No. The Owls are attempting to charge me with …" Her voice trails off. Her gaze darts around and she feels increasingly uncomfortable. It is as though some nefarious spy is eavesdropping on their conversation. Finally, she speaks in a hushed, rapid whisper, "Conspiracy, subverting authority, and I apparently own things outlawed in their Bible. You could be dishonored. You must warn the others. Maybe it is not too late."

Jack looks as if a wasp has stung him. He is speechless for a several moments. Then he replies, "You have to let me help you. It is my responsibility as your friend."

"I know you will aid me, but I must go, *now!* The best help you can give me is by telling the others. All the parents are attending the party, and the Owls might not notice, so go now! I'm headed home."

"I guess you're right, but how can my group be dishonored? If anyone takes a blow to their reputation, it will be me. I asked *you* to be my protector when really *you* are the one who needs protecting." Jack appears desperate.

Serena scrambles to figure out how to get herself out of her precarious situation.

"You will help by telling others. It's too late because the Owls will convict me. You must argue my case at every given opportunity to everyone else," she calmly explains.

She puts her hand on Jack's shoulder. A solitary tear slides down her cheek as she flashes him melancholy smile and then slinks into the stifling darkness, leaving a bewildered Jack on the front porch.

Serena hurries through the night to her house. Annemarie greets her at the door. Sheldon had escorted Serena to the gathering, since his wife had decided to not attend. Annemarie greets her daughter at the door, but Serena wants to get away.

"Did something happen at the party?" Annemarie asks. "I didn't expect you back so early."

"No. Nothing bad happened. I just have a bad headache," Serena lies, masking the urgent edge to her voice while simultaneously cradling her head. Hastily brushing past Annemarie, she hurries to her room and shuts the door. Sitting down on her bed brings the reassuring realization that Mary will remain at the event until the final person leaves for the night. She is relieved that nobody will interrupt her private thoughts. However, Serena's clairvoyant brain fails to account for Annemarie, who calmly swings the door open.

"I know my daughter enough to realize when something in her life has gone wrong," Annemarie says gently. "Let's talk about it."

In a flash of anger, Serena buries her fist into her bed and bursts into furious, frustrated tears. "It doesn't matter. You'll know by tomorrow evening," she sobs.

"What will I know by tomorrow evening? I want to know now."

"Because by tomorrow evening, I will be wandering in the forest, exiled," cries Serena, tears streaming down her face. "At the party, I overheard Anaeus plotting with the Owls to file a denouncement, and Mary was with them. They will approve, and I will be framed."

Annemarie, who finds her temper suddenly rising to volcanic levels, vacates the room. Pure fury swirls in her brain. If Anaeus decides to do this, he will learn the true meaning of being the victim of an angry storm. Meanwhile, Serena tries to comfort herself.

*C'mon. Pull yourself together. It's only one exile. It will pass. You will survive. You have the strength, skill, and common sense to survive.* Reassured, Serena alters her plan from one of winning to one of surviving.

Meanwhile, Annemarie furiously storms over to the church. By this time, a gentle, cool breeze stirs the trees like the waving arms of a crowd. However, Annemarie marches on. The fury ablaze inside her warms her against the chill. Bursting into the church, she walks up to where Anaeus stands talking with his colleagues.

"So, you are planning to exile *my* daughter?" Annemarie demands. Her face is a picture of seriousness, scantily masking her fury.

"Be careful, Annemarie. I have made my decision. Your daughter Serena has broken the law of God and must be punished. You should have kept her in line better," Anaeus replies pointedly, as he had not expected Annemarie's sudden appearance. His mildly irate scowl coveys that her intrusion is not welcome.

Annemarie immediately seizes control of the conversation. Although Anaeus clearly has a height advantage over her, Annemarie is not hindered. She shouts, "You know very well what I am here for. You are going to exile Serena, and I am here to demand you to stop now!"

"That is not for you to dictate." Anaeus indifferently turns back to his conversation with the Owls.

But Annemarie is not done with this argument and refuses to relinquish the trial. Seizing a glass cup, she smashes it against the back of Anaeus's bald, uncovered head. The great crash shatters the conversational atmosphere. Anaeus lurches forward, grasping the back of his head. He violently lurches into a wall and falls to the floor, grunting in deep pain. Shards of glass scatter on the floor. All discourse halts like a surprise traffic jam caused by a crash. Many eyes search to discover the cause of the disturbance, but Annemarie does not care. Turning to the Owls, she vents her fury and berates them.

"I wasn't done speaking to you all. My daughter comes home from this party. She tells me that you were going to *exile* her tomorrow afternoon! What's *more*, you have convinced my *other* daughter, Mary, to help you. Consider this me confronting *you*. Therefore, you will stop this *now*," she demands.

"Annemarie?" exclaims a shocked Sheldon. This development has surprised him like a nobleman looted by Robin Hood.

Anaeus straightens himself. Titus nervously pats the back of Anaeus's head with a napkin.

"Serena chose her own path. Now she will face the consequences of those choices. These matters do not concern you," Josephus states firmly.

Annemarie continues berating the Owls. "If something concerns *my daughter*, it *is* my business. Whose daughter is Serena? *Mine* or *yours*? Because last I checked, *I* gave birth to Serena, *I* raised her, and *I'm* going to do what's right for *her*."

Annemarie continues, focusing her attention on Titus. "Listen here, you, you might be the head pastor and in charge of the people's faith, but last I checked, I gave birth to Serena, and I raised Serena to be a woman who loves God with everything she has. However, it is apparent that nobody in this room believes that."

"There is nothing you can do, Annemarie. Justice will be carried out. You have failed as a mother," Titus says, returning her anger with his own controlled fury.

"You've always been against me. You have been plotting to take my joy. This is why I wanted to leave this godforsaken town. I don't know why I even chose to live in this place when I know God has left here. You are my enemies! You are my Satan! Now get behind me." Annemarie storms on. In her younger years, she'd had a combative and aggressive personality. Proof of that is once again before their eyes.

"You are out of line! Remove yourself from our presence now!" bellows Oceanus, recovering his composure.

Annemarie refuses to wait for them to conclude their arguments. She angrily marches home before the stunned crowd can attempt any action against her.

Mary also remains stunned into surprised silence by her mother's actions. A few minutes later, Sheldon collects his second-eldest daughter to take her home. The night gradually grows colder, and Mary wishes she had brought her light coat as she and Sheldon and trudge back to the house.

On their way, Sheldon sparks a conversation. "Thank you for coming home with me. I'm sorry we had to leave early, but I'm needed at home."

Mary does not accept her father's thanks in words. "Why, Father? Why did Mother act like that in front of everyone?"

"Your mother loves you and your sister and would do anything for you. This time Serena needs your mother's help, and your mother is doing her best to protect Serena."

Mary sighs and tries to reassure herself. *It does not matter what happens. The denouncement will be filed, the hearing will take place, and Serena will be exiled tomorrow.* Yet the words feel empty.

Mary wonders about this until Sheldon says in between deep breaths, "This is when unity matters, especially among our family. Watch, Mary. In the coming weeks, Anaeus will regret sending Serena into exile. This is what happens when our family and the church are divided. Satan has that strength. He knows what will divide us Christians, and that is what Satan is doing right now through Anaeus and the Owls."

When Sheldon and Mary arrive home, Mary ascends the stairs to her room. She shakes her head, thinking, *Great. Now my position is so much more complicated because of my role in Serena's trial. They will know by tomorrow. I have made a great mistake.*

CHAPTER 13

# TRIALS AND EXILES

The sun rises on Sunday, bright and cheery, but to Serena, gloomy clouds and rain are in the forecast. She barely touches her breakfast, and it grows cold. Her mind is unfocused during the church service. She allows a single scoffing smile when she contemplates how Mary will be helping her accusers.

She forces herself to eat a light lunch and dons her typical T-shirt and overalls. But this time, she puts on her new swimsuit under her usual attire and slips her pocketknife, a piece of flint, and a striker down the front of her shirt. She securely fastens them in place with a fishing line and hook. The metal and stone feel cold where the smuggled tools lie against her chest.

Serena does not fear the survival aspect of exile. She knows every plant in the region and its useful properties. She is also a veteran hunter with an alert mindset. However, she dreads the dreary loneliness that lurks like an evil spirit. Thus, she fears and hates the idea of lone survival. She is emotionally defeated.

Throughout the early afternoon, Serena's brain replays every ill-fated incident between her and Anaeus, to her annoyance. Will a defaming trial and expulsion into the forest mark her downfall? She will not allow that to happen.

The time for the trail finally arrives. Serena walks to the church and stands in the defendant area. It's an open wooden platform about three feet by three feet with a space that leads into one of the back hallways. Elaborate carvings from different scenes in the Bible adorn its thick walls. These quarters may only come up to her waist, but she deems escape impossible because this position makes any person on trial extremely visible to the audience sitting in the pews.

Yellow flowers decorate the church sanctuary. Serena watches people steadily file in as singles and groups. She cannot help but think, *how ironic. My accusers are cowards. They will refuse to debate me with valid charges and must invent sins to lay at my door.*

Serena spots Jack in the crowd and motions for him to approach. She leans precariously over the rim of her open confinement. He comes over, and the pair hold a public but hushed conversation.

"It is as I feared," Serena whispers. "I will be exiled because of these accusations."

"How could they convict someone as witty as you? I have come to know that you are a master when it comes to words and wit. You can turn their arguments into foolishness," Jack says as quietly as he can.

Serena senses the unbelief that is raging like a besieging army battering against the gate of quietness in his voice.

"The Owls hate me, and they have wanted a good reason to remove me from their perfect society." Serena looks off toward where Anaeus stands conversing with the other Owls. "And now they have that reason," she says in disgust.

"But surely you could pull something off? Something massive! Try getting the crowd on your side!" Jack speaks frantically, stuttering the entire time.

"I wish I could, but I am not God. I can't control the Owls. He would have to personally approach the Owls in order for me to attain victory here today." She hangs her head in resignation at the only thing that can remedy her situation. Her speckled locks veil her face.

"But why would God do something like this? It does not feel like his style to allow bad things to happen," Jack says.

"First, this feels like God's way. He uses our bad situations to bring us closer to him, but often for another purpose. However, it shall remain elusive until God wishes otherwise. You must remember, I am suffering because of other people's choices, not yours. This is not a punishment but a test, for you and for me. Except I believe that I can—"

Serena is forced to abandon speaking as Anaeus calls everyone to order and begins a speech to set the context of the hearing. Jack retreats to his original post beside his mother, Mariah. The way Anaeus states the facts makes Serena appear guilty. The speech ends when he calls Toby and Mary to stand and bids them to tell what they know, or in this case what the Owls tell them to say.

Toby clears his throat and begins his elaborate speech. "Yes, Anaeus. Thank you for this opportunity to speak on behalf of this argument now." He momentarily pauses to clear his throat.

Mary stands by his side with a serious scowl on her face. But Serena does not care about facial expressions at this moment.

"Yes. So where should we begin? There are many possible places to start. Oh, yes. I know. I was attending the party last night, enjoying some conversation with my peers. Serena was there too. I do not know if she came willingly or if she was forced. However, I believe she was not enjoying it. I saw her eat something, but she sat alone. Presently, the Owls arose and went to discuss some private business. Serena followed them. I saw her getting an unfilled glass. After that, I knew that she was going to try to spy on the Owls. My friend Mary here has mastered that trade, so she knows what to look for."

At that point, Toby motions to Mary, who curtsies slightly. Serena stares at the pair. Meanwhile, Toby speeds up his testimony.

"I decided to follow Serena and see what she was up to. I don't believe she saw me. I saw her place the glass against the door of the room the Owls had gone into. However, she did not remain there very long. She jumped away from the door, clearly scared by something. At this point, I retreated to my table, as I feared discovery. I told everyone there about what I saw. Right after Serena left, the Owls and Mary came out of the room. Mary came over to my table."

"Who was at your table?" Titus asks, attempting to draw out every detail.

"A handful of her friends. However, they were in a separate conversation and did not hear me," Toby replies.

"And, Mary, can you confirm this?" Titus asks.

"Yes, I can. I was there." Mary's voice sounds cold like low bell tones on a freezing day.

*At least Jack is safe and won't get into trouble. I must not involve him,* Serena thinks. However, the next part of Toby's speech dashes all hopes concerning Jack's well-being.

"I connected this event to a past event where I observed Jack, Lawrence, and Stephanie going together into the belfry. I followed them up to the belfry. I thought that I could catch some of the conversation. Nobody saw me, because it was very dark. I kept track of them by following the sound of their footsteps. The three ahead of me were making a racket. I'm surprised someone below didn't hear them. Anyway, they reached the bell tower, and the three climbed up to the actual bell. There's a metal ladder there. I got a good look at it in the moonlight. I remained below and listened. I heard them talking about a friendship. However, the voice answering wasn't Stephanie. This puzzled me since I had only seen three. I was determined to find out who this fourth person was. I overheard the smacking of hands like someone was shaking on a deal. I immediately descended, fearing my discovery. Nobody came with me, so I can't provide more proof. I immediately told Titus about the intruders in the belfry. I did not know who the fourth intruder was. I suspected Serena because of her late arrival. I saw her sit with Alexia, Penny, and Sarah. After the party, I asked Penny about Serena, and she told me that she had been the fourth intruder."

Serena cringes as if stabbed by a knife.

"Furthermore, I also have evidence of her deep ties to Jack and his group of friends. She has often gone with them into the forest. I don't know what he does or what Serena has planned in the future, but I believe she is up to no good. She is a mastermind of evil. You spied on the Owls because you feared you were caught before your scheme could be carried out," Toby concludes.

Serena knows her past record contains countless misdeeds. However, Toby strings her life into a serious-looking conspiracy. Her thoughts are interrupted when she glances at the audience and notices Annemarie beginning to stand up.

"Oh no you don't," protests one resident.

"After what you did last night to Anaeus, Annemarie, you are not fit to interrupt these proceedings," another complains.

"Sheldon, will you take your wife away? She is in contempt of court," Anaeus demands.

Sheldon glares at him before whispering something into her ear, and the pair slowly walk out of the sanctuary. With Serena's parents gone, Anaeus asks his second question.

"And, Mary, I understand you also have a story to tell?"

"Yes. Before the party, I found Serena with one of those immodest swimsuits. I naturally confronted her about her sin, but Serena threatened me, took my hairpin, and told me she would accuse me of disturbing her."

Serena shakes her head slightly sending strands of hair to brush against her shoulders and fall down her face. as if to say, "You had to use that to incriminate me." sending strands of her hair to brush against her shoulders.

At this revelation, the crowd transforms into a roaring lion, declaring that Serena should not have the chance to defend herself. During the time of Toby and Mary's verbal onslaught, Serena remains sitting on the provided chair at the far end of the defendant area. Her legs are crossed, and her hands are clasped in her lap in a dignified manner. She does not move or speak the entire time. A solitary tear slips down her face.

When she finally speaks, a handful of people remember her words twenty years later. "God forgive you. That is all that is worth saying."

The crowd seems struck dumb. Nobody utters a word. Except for Anaeus, who bellows to his audience, "The jury will now deliberate! May God reveal the guilty party!"

The Owls exit the room from the choir berths, where they have been sitting for the trial.

Jack hurries over to the defendant box, and he and Serena hold another whispered conversation.

"What kind of defense was that?" Jack asks.

"That wasn't a defense. The Owls would have convicted me if I had spoken for eight hours as opposed to the four seconds I used."

"I thought you could still use the fact that the Owls are perpetrating this lie."

"In good time, eventually the lies will be seen as lies, and it will come back against them," Serena says.

"I will pray for you."

"Thank you, Jack. I'm going to need it."

Serena watches Jack retreat from the church and notices the team do the same. Thus, all of Serena's friends scatter like the disciples in Gethsemane. She sees Stephanie vacating the sanctuary. Lawrence's arm settles on her shoulders. Serena knows now she is alone.

It feels as if only a few seconds have passed when the Owls file back to announce the verdict.

"We declare the defendant guilty, and we, as the governmental body of this current establishment, exile you, Serena."

The sound is deafening for the surrendered Serena, who winces at every word. Two ruddy, burly, strong-looking attendants named Gideon and Aaron dutifully blaze their way to the defendant area. They bind her wrists. Serena doesn't resist and voluntarily places her arms together. She attempts to steal a final sad look at those who wrought her demise. Anaeus, Mary, and Toby glare at her with distain from their powerful positions. With another look into the audience, she sees Mariah smiling in jubilation and applauding Anaeus's decision. With a sharp tug on the rope, the two attendants briskly march Serena from the room.

Aaron and Gideon lead her through town, past the school, the houses, even the meat processing plant. A dangerous mob follows. They hurl insults and declare that God will punish her, but Serena is deaf to their slander and does not say a word. A massive weight has been thrust upon her shoulders. It feels like a cross.

Finally, Gideon and Aaron stomp out of the village and into the forest. The mob disperses and people drift back to their daily life, though Serena still senses eyes watching from the woodsy shadows. The attendants escort Serena past the familiar swimming holes and down another path that continues to the north. They pass a sign that says, "No hunting beyond this point. Thank you." However, Serena is preoccupied with a realization: *Anaeus did not say how long I am to stay in exile.*

They come upon a shallow, gurgling river, where the path transforms into a worn bridge. Serena patiently holds her arms out as they are unbound, and she does not move or complain as they pat down her sides and check her pockets for smuggled survival gear. After escorting her across the bridge, they walk away. Serena remains standing where she has been left for several moments. A final tear slips down her disheartened, weary face, and she turns away.

"And so my new life begins." Serena sighs as she plunges into the dense woodland beyond the river.

Eventually overcome by exhaustion, she collapses to the ground. The gathering dust contrasts with shadows, making Serena's skin glow red like a warrior pierced by many wounds. Her mouth contorts into a painful grimace, and she clutches a stick in her fist like a sword. The enemy has won this battle, but he will have to face a determined opponent in the next to win the war.

## CHAPTER 14

# SETTLING DOWN, PART 1

When the sun rises the next day, Serena wakes sore, stiff, and groaning. She shakes her head groggily, momentarily clearing the tiredness that nearly glues her to the ground. She feels dirty and like insects had crawled on her. As she stands, she feels painful pangs of hunger and hears the low, gurgling rumble of her stomach. The suspense and impending doom from yesterday clearly affected her.

"Are you kidding me!" Serena shouts to the forest.

Birds shoot into the sky with a shrill melody of surprised chirps and fearful squawks. Serena lifts her fist into the air as if to curse the world in defiance. It is as if some inner voice flips a switch, accessing her abilities as a survivalist.

A glance around the forest floor shows a carpet of green plants of different shapes and sizes. Thorns protrude from some, while others have none. As Serena scans the undergrowth, her stomach groans again.

"I'm not desperate. I'm not desperate. I have prepared for this moment," Serena repeats to herself despite the sinking hopeless feeling creeping in. She begins to walk forward with slow, efficient steps to conserve her energy. She relies on her eyes to find something easy to eat.

Her eyes spot a blackberry bush. She descends upon it and feasts on its fruit. As she explores further, she observes several blackberry bushes near the shore of the little stream. Upon discovering these, the exile's stomach grumbles incessantly. Normally at home, she would have eaten breakfast much earlier. To add to her distress, she did not have dinner yesterday. Thus, Serena gorges on the blackberries, and the purple juice stains her hands.

With her stomach temporarily satisfied, she begins to plot her next move. She sits against the rough bark of an oak tree and broodingly stares into the wilderness. The forest sounds and the distant gurgle of the river surround her, breaking the solitude. Until her stomach begins to grumble again.

Serena reasons that, since fruits have sugar as their primary nutrient, the insulin release quickly has made her hungry again. She slowly rises, berating herself for not eating a large lunch or breakfast before her trial. She sets off walking, following the quiet flow of the river.

She emerges from the forest at a spot in the river where the bank is not steep and branches into an incredibly shallow but muddy swamp. The first signs are the hollow stalks and brown tops of cattails. She retrieves a stick from the woods to scout the ground so it will not collapse on her. Serena grabs the stalk of the nearest cattail. Then, reaching down to the muddy ground, she lifts, uprooting the plant, knowing its roots, shoots, and stalks are quite edible if cooked right. Using her stick to probe the ground ahead of her, she makes it to shore after harvesting two more cattails.

Upon reaching the shore, Serena sets to work cutting the stalks into four-inch sections. Then she peels away the layers of the stalk to take her appetite out upon the starchy cores. She feasts away, devouring the cattail stalks so quickly she almost chokes on the fibers. The starch satisfies her stomach.

Serena leaves her place by the river and methodically maneuvers through the complicated, twisted maze of plants and thorns of the forest. The day is peaceful and sunny with a sympathetic sun gracing the sky. Trees cause rays to cast stripes of light upon the forest floor. Eventually, Serena emerges from the dense covering of the forest to discover a small canyon. Standing at the tallest point, Serena admires it from above.

The canyon is not deep, but many massive boulders stick out of the hillside and caves dot the gaps between them. Some appear to burrow deep into the hillside, while others look like little divots in the earth. However, these details do not draw the same interest from her as the stream that trickles and bubbles over the rocky canyon bottom. Small plant life populates the area, forming a thick green mist that can be seen everywhere. Petite saplings struggle to stay alive in the rocky outcroppings. Larger trees that kill the ground cover can never survive here. A substantial number of boulders are piled together and pushed into one corner. Serena mentally eliminates that corner as a suitable choice for shelter because she fears she could be killed if those rocks tumble down, and survival is everything at this moment.

Serena selects this canyon as her base of operations and journeys down into the rocky place. After a delicate search heavily impeded by plant life, she chooses a promising divot that extends an adequate eight feet into the hillside to serve as her main living quarters. She considers other caves as useful for storage rooms. But Serena has underestimated how much brush is crammed inside the canyon. Every crevice that is not clogged the by rocky soil is occupied a sprawling bush, rendering easy mobility nearly impossible. Her slow descent is punctuated by frequent rests to plan how to navigate the undergrowth. She continually makes detours to avoid the clingy mangle of thorns growing along the steep path down. The path appears to have been used many years ago, but most evidence has been erased like the ruins of ancient cities destroyed in biblical times.

The forest around the canyon dims the forest floor with a dark hue. In many places, the brambles, thorn bushes, thistles, Virginia creeper, poison ivy, and countless other unidentifiable vegetation cast shadows. Although her ability to maneuver in and out of the canyon is hindered, Serena now believes that everything she needs to survive in the wilderness exists right here. She has fresh water for cooking and drinking.

With her stomach somewhat satisfied, Serena commences transforming her cave into a place where she can reside. First, she wants the rocky floor to be made more comfortable. In the past, she remembers camping trips. Normally, she would pack a sleeping bag or hammock, but she could not take them to the trial to carry into exile. Dejected, Serena slumps down on a rock to think.

"C'mon, think. How do you solve this problem? If you had forgotten your sleeping bag, what would you use instead?" Serena asks herself. "I don't know, maybe I could try to spread some fresh leaves on the floor and that might be a bit more comfortable."

Thus, Serena embarks on an experiment so she will be more comfortable tonight. Scrambling out of the canyon, she assembles a considerable cache of firewood and berries. With that task completed, her stomach starts to run on fumes again.

In response, Serena fashions a rod from one of the branches she cut down and attaches the string that concealed her smuggled items, constructing a crude fishing pole. She also adheres to the fishing commandment, "Thou shalt not use bait from any store," by turning over some rocks near the shore, searching for worms or anything else to use for bait. Then, selecting one of the bigger pools in the stream, she casts her line.

Within a few moments, Serena flips a small bluegill onto the rocky bank. It flops around until one swift blow with a light, sharp stone ends its life. Summoning her knife, Serena cleans the fish and flays its stomach. She wants to investigate the creature's diet. Noticing the emptiness, she opportunistically casts again and retrieves another three fish in the next five minutes.

With that done, Serena finds a large rock, places her catch upon it, and loosens up the dirt with a stick to build a fire. Next, she starts a small fire, encouraging it to grow by feeding it twigs and others small dry tinder. Once the fire reaches a good size, Serena places a large rock in the middle of it, which will take a long time to heat up. While waiting and maintaining the fire, she gathers a large pile of leaves to make a large nest to sleep by the river. Arranging the nest takes a long time, especially since Serena wants the fresh leaves that have not been on the ground. As she works, Serena focuses on the job and becomes less hungry. By the end, her hands are tired and the hunger pangs are settling strongly in her stomach.

She checks on the rock in the middle of the flames and nearly burns her finger. She gathers the fish, places them on the rock to cook, watching them hungrily. After a few minutes, she selects a forklike stick and flips the fish one by one. They sizzle as the juices on the other sides fry. At length, Serena carefully lifts the fish onto a flat cold rock and sets about cleaning the flakey treats of scales. Then she finally sets on her feast and eats ravenously.

That night, Serena sleeps on a nest of fresh leaves.

CHAPTER 15

# REBELS

While Serena establishes herself in the forest, a different situation develops in Christville. The Owls start a relief organization. They call this assembly the Young Men's Relief Program (YMRP) as a Christian aid program. Although Anaeus creates it, Toby is appointed the leader, a position that he gleefully accepts.

To start, Toby outlaws Jack's football games. Second, he alienates the protectors, saying they can never fall for the women's tricks again. Finally, he forbids venturing into the forest. Toby reasons that none of his members can place themselves in vulnerable positions. Thereby, he makes it completely illegal to do anything the young men of Christville normally do in summer. Anaeus also grants Toby the power to exile members of the YMRP for one day. Toby is even more excited by this, and he orders the boys in his organization to salute in his presence or be exiled.

And so, the YMRP slowly wraps its controlling fingers around every young man in Christville. One by one, members of Jack's group are pressured, coerced, or forced to join.

Jack and Perceval are the last to not have placed their signatures on the YMRP's registry. The pair have heard reports about the YMRP from members of Jack's football team. His former players complain about the organization's rules and that Toby has absolutely no authority to declare himself a leader in anything. They call the YMRP totalitarian and recommend to anyone who has not joined to not consider joining at all.

Today, Jack and Perceval are hanging out in Jack's bedroom. His room is located on the upper story of his house, and he shares it with his second-oldest brother, James, who is currently hiding in the forest from Toby. Both of their beds are pushed against a window, confirming the room's structural location in a corner of the house. At the foot of each bed, a desk contains the various trinkets that collect over the years. White sunlight illuminates patches of the room and reflects off airborne dust particles. Shadows abound but remain in their customary places. The floor is a short carpet, while the walls are painted a peachy color and are without ornament. A medium-sized light hangs over the room but is not on.

Jack sits on his bed. Perceval looks sullenly at him from where he sits in the desk chair. Being denounced and exiled is the worst punishment anyone can face, and now Toby is allowed to abuse it. To Jack's group, it is the worst-case scenario. All that tragedy had befallen Jack's beautiful protector, Serena, and it is negatively impacting the rest of his group.

In the silence, Jack tries to sort his scattered thoughts of recent events. *Why wouldn't Serena defend herself? I thought Serena was smart. I have failed. I was not loyal to her, and now Serena has been exiled, and Toby stinks.*

Perceval rises to morosely to return home. At least the crowds that used to track him all over Christville have disappeared. Since he and Jack are considered bad company, people have gone on their way. He turns to leave and tells Jack what is on his mind.

"Why don't you start another organization to combat Toby's? We should fight against him and the evil he represents!" Perceval sounds so excited to combat Toby.

"I-I don't know," Jack stutters. "I need to think."

"Jack, would you let Toby get away with his rules and his way?" Perceval demands.

"Yes, you are right, but still. Let me think of a better way," Jack stammers, still searching for his voice, or mind, or maybe both.

Perceval speaks persuasively, displaying a high intelligence and vocabulary. Jack knows from experience that this means Perceval is trying to convince him to do something.

"If you lead, lots of guys will be with you one hundred percent! We'll make Toby a leader without followers!" Perceval says enthusiastically.

Jack lets out a melancholy sigh. "I like the support that you are showing me. I appreciate it. But a rebellion is not what I want right now," he tells his friend. His mind returns to the present. "If you and the others want to go and start, then I must delay it. I want to think first."

"Many are demanding action right away. They may not like your answer." Perceval sounds concerned.

"People have not liked the decisions made in recent days. People in my group have not liked some of the decisions I have made. I have no power over them. The Bible says that we should obey and respect those in authority whether that person in authority is a liar, a trickster, or a cheat," Jack says. "If any want to take action, I will not support them for now."

"Your followers will hate this."

"I know of many unpopular leaders. I, myself, have been hated by others at times," Jack says with false-fronted confidence.

However, Perceval catches a lingering, indecisive tone in his leader's voice. He sadly departs for home. He does not visit Jack the next day, but Perceval's words are burned into Jack's scattered mind. Instead of immediately plotting a course for the safety of the forest, Jack aimlessly wanders Christville's streets.

*We'll make Toby a leader. Without followers.* The words eerily echo in his mind.

As he wanders, Jack happens upon a group of players from the football team. He raises his hand as a silent greeting and initiates conversation.

"Say, Jack, would it be all right if we simply rebelled against Toby? What he has been doing is outrageous," Arthur says.

Jack ponders Arthur's question before answering. The others wait impatiently.

"At the moment, I have not decided. Yes, Toby is not doing good things to us, but the answer is not simply rebelling against him. There is more to this situation than that."

"How come? As far as I can tell, Toby is the person giving the orders. He should be the one slighted," says Arthur, who has evidently accepted the task of speaking for the group.

"Because Toby is appointed by Anaeus, and Toby is making the rules in Anaeus's name. Therefore, rebelling against Toby does not address the root issue," Jack explains.

Arthur nods, appearing to accept Jack's argument. However, the crowd behind the pair rumbles in complaint. Just then, Perceval walks up to the front of the crowd from where he had been hiding in the back.

"C'mon, guys. We don't need to listen to Jack here when all we need to do is ignore what Toby says. C'mon. Who's with me?" Perceval shouts, projecting his voice so everyone in the crowd can hear.

"C'mon. Be reasonable. You won't accomplish anything from this. The only result you will get is exile for a day. Then you do something to Toby, and he exiles you again. It's a complete cycle of pointlessness," Jack argues. His voice begins to waver as the disapproving gazes of his teammates bear down on him. "If we are to resist Toby, Toby can't notice us doing it, so why bother?"

"Jack's idea takes longer to think up and longer to execute. I will bring about immediate results," Perceval says.

"Yeah. I agree with Perceval," Tomas yells.

"I too," shouts another player named David.

Eventually, the players gather around Perceval, and they march down the street, leaving Jack alone, or so he thinks.

Lawrence stays behind, watching the large group go. He turns to Jack, whose face is stoically pointed toward the ground. The two stand together in silence.

Then Jack notices his friend's presence and says, "What about you, Lawrence?"

"I've made up my mind. I'm siding with you."

"What? Why?"

"Well, you see, you've been my friend for a while, so I thought I should stick with you."

"Thanks, Lawrence. That means a lot," Jack whispers.

Despite Toby not allowing Jack or any members of his group into the forest, Jack and Lawrence spend the next hour in the forest, talking and walking the paths. Then the two go home to think about what to do about Toby.

The next day finds Jack withdrawn into his mind, waging the same war of disbelief and shock that besieges him. Voices creep into his mind like worms into a moldy apple. It feels as though all the devils in the world have decided to converge on him.

They crowd around him whispering, "God does not care for you. If he did, then Serena would have won out when they denounced her."

Jack can sense their presence.

Instead of readily giving in to their temptations, Jack does not hesitate to shoot back his own reply, which blows with the force of a trumpet: "God has a different plan. I must endure."

"Do you know what God's plan exactly is?"

"No, but I don't need to know," Jack replies. His determination wavers slightly.

In return, the enemies pounce like a lion on their prey. "If you do not know what God's plan is, then how do you know that God will rescue you? Will Serena ever leave her exile? What if she is forever cast out, never to return?" The uncertainty they introduce creates a plague of doubt within Jack's mind. An answer becomes as possible as flying to Jack. However, the army of ravenous lions continue their barrage.

"Why don't you ask God about his plan? If he answers you, then he must have some shred of kindness for you. If he doesn't, then he must not care for you."

Jack possesses no words to make the request or to argue. He freezes, stuck in the mud of indecision. His mind tears at the invisible opponent, dreaming of brutalizing Toby for his lies and trickery. Except when one side of his imagination finishes with the image, his logic instantly rends it to pieces, saying, *Toby has the Owls on his side. I should try to act normal. Or at least be more discreet about my resistance.*

Meanwhile, the battle against the hostile lions intensifies. "You want to be the leader. Your former position as the leader of the football team, you want to regain it. We can give it to you. It could be all yours. All that is required of you is to eliminate Toby and the Owls, and then nobody would dare accuse or dishonor you in any way again. You may even become an Owl. All you need to do is give in to your anger. Take your revenge."

The pressure upon Jack mounts as numerous propositions of ranging variables of resistance overwhelmingly crowd his stressed mind. Jack needs to decide before his squad openly rebels against Toby. His imagination is not required to dwell on the result. Though he has the capabilities of a leader, opposition is an alien from an unknown planet.

"What is your answer?" demand the devils, circling him like an army besieging a fortress, intent on crushing him.

How can he combat the idea of a glorious revolution compared with the dull and humiliating reality that incessantly haunts him. Should he accept the idea of doing nothing? Except Jack remains strong against the unending attack, and the enemy finds himself pushed back.

"I never thought or believed Serena could be found guilty or exiled because of those crimes. Christians help those who can't help themselves. I will do everything to rescue Serena from her exile. I will counsel Perceval against action without thought and lift those who need comfort. This is how we resist Toby, not in battle but in service."

At this, the devils deem Jack an impossible fortress. They abandon their positions and flee.

The door of Jack's room creaks open, and Mariah Irving walks in. Jack looks away. Mrs. Irving is taller than Annemarie but still shorter than most men living in Christville. Her skin is a healthy olive hue, and her hair is blacker than a region affected by a full solar eclipse.

"Hi, Jack. How are you?" Mariah kisses Jack's forehead and places her hand on his back.

"Uh, fine," Jack says. "What have you come to talk with me about?"

"I came here to talk about your late friend Serena," Mariah says. "This is really going to be hard for me to say, but now that Serena is gone, I want you to find another girl. You know that I don't approve of Serena."

"Why can't I still be friends with Serena even if she's in exile? I know you don't like her, but I still want to be friends with her."

Mariah sighs and turns to gaze out Jack's window. She clenches and unclenches her fist. "Jack, Serena is illegitimate. Credit to Pastor Sheldon for marrying Annemarie even if she did not deserve it. But Sheldon is still not her father, and I don't want you to associate with her company."

Now it is Jack's turn to be silent. He didn't know Serena was born out of wedlock. He struggles to contemplate how the timeline of his protector's life fits in with that of her parents.

"I don't care about how Serena was born or who her parents really were. I have been working hard to build a relationship with her. I care about her, and I want her to return safely."

"Fine then. Go and see where this takes you." Irritated, Mariah vacates the room. Jack sighs again, still struggling with Mariah's revelation.

CHAPTER 16

# SETTLING DOWN, PART 2

**D**ays and weeks flutter by like the mist in the forest. Life in an inhospitable forest deals a naturally terrible hand to Serena. The weather turns oppressively humid, tiresomely pushing its watery force upon all creatures in the region. While her smuggled knife, flint, striker, and one small fishing hook ease the difficulty, challenges constantly contest Serena's chances of survival.

Serena gradually develops a daily routine. Upon waking, she rebuilds the fire to cook. Then she catches river fish for breakfast. She spends the remainder of her morning searching for wood and satisfying the unquenchable appetite of the fire. She scrounges the forest for different greens and berries to make a simple salad for a light lunch and continually gathers wood.

After lunch, Serena knows she has many other tasks. Her dinner is comprised of fish because of its abundance. One day, Serena uncovers river mussels and cooks them for dinner for variety. She improves her shelter in the waning hours of the day, which ends with an uncomfortable sleep next to her small fire. Then Serena wakes, sore from the pine boughs that form her mattress, to catch more fish. Serena lives as a scavenger.

However, she has three natural enemies that oppose her. The first is the heat and humidity. During the hottest part of the day, she often searches for a shady crevasse to escape the afternoon heat. She also constructs a shelter to protect her from the humidity.

The other enemy that the humidity brings is mosquitos with their affinity for watery heat and shady spots. They make her life uncomfortable, and she finds herself under constant attack. The battle against them frustratingly intensifies as Serena must cope with them while she tries to sleep at night.

The third enemy Serena battles is the rain, and she hates it the most. The weather has been humid and rainy, and frequent deluges drench every stick, leaf, rock, and twig. Serena finds her shelter inadequate at holding back the rain. So, she continues to seek better shelter in the cramped divots or the misleading caves, which do not offer much protection if a slight breeze meanders through the canyon during a rainstorm. Often when the rain begins to fall, she finds herself huddled inside a divot, bedraggled and uncomfortable. At least the insects do not bother her during a rainstorm.

However, life does not always bully her in the forest. For example, she works hard for her primary food sources of fish, edible plants, and berries, but she knows that it is just enough to sustain her throughout her exile.

After the first two weeks in the forest as an exile, Serena decides to go exploring to break the monotony of her regular routine. After gathering her precious belongings, she strides into the forest. For a while, she aimlessly treks through the forest, admiring its green beauty. She has not gone far beyond the canyon since the day she was cast from town. The sound of the river gurgles in the distance. Then, turning down a small deer track, she finds a swimming hole.

This swimming hole is nestled inside a rocky outcropping trussed together by the exposed root system of a towering tree. The rocks retain a glossy surface. Green moss and slimy skin coat them. At one end, a massive boulder juts out over the deepest part, making a type of shallow area. For a while, Serena stands at the brink, admiring the still, clear water. Then, removing everything except her swimsuit and throwing her clothes on top of a rock, she jumps in. For several minutes, she enjoys herself, wading, swimming, and just plain soaking. Eventually, she climbs out and blissfully relaxes on the mossy rock as the air dries her hair. She stays there until the sun starts to go to bed.

Serena recalls the most cited rule in the survivalist's handbook: never be caught away from your home or shelter at night. She collects her few possessions and scampers away into the approaching night.

Some might call her life crude, but she never voices her complaints. In fact, she hardly ever speaks at all. Life solemnly marches on. Many rainstorms, damp days, and downpours follow. Sometimes thunder lets loose its low rumble, and on other occasions, it crashes across the sky, alerting the entire world to its presence. Yet Serena endures as she has done before.

CHAPTER 17

# PERFECTIONISTS

Since Serena's exile two weeks ago, Jack begins to work for longer periods of time at his job at the diner. He wakes at 5:30 a.m. to exercise rigorously and lift weights before preparing for his shift at 7:00 a.m. However, despite his best efforts, his mind overflows with images of Serena, imprisoning him in a semi depressed state. He dwells on the events from two weeks ago. Despite Jack's pledge to aid his protector, he is not sure how to help.

After exercising, Jack dresses in his work uniform, which is a pale collared shirt and black pants. He normally keeps his midnight-blue apron at the diner. He marches solemnly down the morning streets to the diner. It is cloudy, and the humidity feels like Christians' burden.

The diner occupies a modest single-story structure with a massive front window. It has a white brick wall with blue trim, giving it an iconic appearance. Jack saunters down an adjacent alley that the garbage truck trundles down to collect the restaurant's refuse. He locates the emergency key and unlocks the side door to the restaurant.

Jack enters the dark building and turns on the lights, illuminating an empty kitchen. A large stove stands idle at one end. On the opposite end, a large metal sink and dishwasher sleep in the corner.

Plates are neatly stacked in an open cupboard. Cooking utensils, dishrags, and meal trays line the various shelves and counters that fill up the rest of the space along one edge. A large silver refrigerator remains the sole object on duty. To the side of that, a steel gray door marks the entrance to the large walk-in freezer.

Jack sighs and trudges over to the industrial dishwasher. He looks inside. It's empty. Mutely, he settles down on the sturdy counter and waits.

A large *boom* shatters his thoughts. The sky growls. Rain pelts the streets. Jack hurries to the door and latches it behind him. The alley has instantly transformed into a squishy mud bath. Jack glumly glances at the ticking clock. It is too early to open. Jack wanders into the lobby where all customers eat. Leaning on the cashier's desk, he stares into an imaginary abyss.

This area in the diner sports the most outlandish items in Christville. The checkered tables are customized with two drawers built into each. One drawer contains chess pieces and the other checkers. Additionally, along one wall is a modest set of arcade games. Battleship Galactica, Dig Dug, Pac Man, and two pinball tables provide the primary excitement. Kids enjoy the devices for their inside activities. Little boys constantly compete for the highest scores.

The sound of someone banging at the back door brings Jack back to reality. Jack hastens to unlock the door, and swings it open. Lawrence stands in the mud on the other side, wearing his soaked uniform, minus the apron.

"Well, aren't you going to let me in? The rain's pelting down," demands an indignant, bedraggled Lawrence.

Jack steps aside to allow the disheveled employee entrance. Lawrence walks past Jack and tosses a towel over his head. He shoots an aggressive glare at Jack.

"I don't suppose you'd feel like heading home now," Jack says.

"I don't know. I've attracted more water than a dog after a bath," Lawrence replies crossly. He places more dishrags on the counter before sitting on them. "Do you think it's time to open the restaurant?" he asks after a lengthy silence.

"No. Plus, I haven't seen Mr. Stanton at all, and I wouldn't open the store without his permission." Jack strolls over to the counter facing the lobby and attempts to sit down.

The creak of a door sounds from the back of the store. Jack startles, and Lawrence falls off the counter.

"What in the world and tarnation was that?" Lawrence looks around the kitchen for someone he missed.

"Relax, Lawrence. It's only me," shouts a voice from the other side of the kitchen.

The owner of the restaurant, Mr. Stanton, lumbers into view. He has a squat figure with tanned skin, a pot belly, and short, stocky arms and legs. Only a little portion of gray fuzz occupies the crown of his head, and a fuzzy, gray, caterpillar-like mustache slithers across the space between his nose and upper lip. He wears the same white shirt as Jack and Lawrence, blue jeans, and a messy, old, stained apron. His eyes are an intense blue and sparkle with joy when he laughs. His clothes are also wet and clinging to his skin.

The wet uniform irritates him. He grumbles, "There are enough bad moods in this world fer yuh ta be glowerin' about the place."

Meanwhile, Lawrence hoists himself up from the floor and brushes his hands off on his jeans as if they had contracted some kind of dust. "Why did you have to scare me? I thought someone had broken in."

Mr. Stanton ignores the question. Alternately, he beckons the pair to a table. "Let's brighten everyone's mood fer tuday."

Jack and Lawrence hurry to prepare the game. Thunder rumbles in the distance. Rain slashes at the windows. The wind shrieks and moans in the building's chimneys while the trio play checkers and chess. The trio soon become a quartet when Tomas, Mr. Stanton's eldest son, joins them. Upon Tomas's arrival, Mr. Stanton announces a grand checkers and chess tournament, despite the lack of audience.

At length, Mr. Stanton whimsically dismantles Jack for the

third consecutive time in chess. On any other day, Jack contends with the best players of the sport, despite his immense love of football.

"Jack, why yuh lookin' like a patch o' dyin' flowers when yuh come ta work every day?" Mr. Stanton asks.

"The past two weeks have been rough." Jack stares into the violent storm outside.

"That's no answer," replies Mr. Stanton. "Fer the past couple o' weeks you've been a comin' tuh work lookin' like you've been tuh a dumb funeral."

"It's about Serena's hearing and exile two weeks ago. We've become good friends over the past nine months, but the Owls didn't approve of her. Toby and Mary denounced her, and since the Owls were behind the accusation, she lost the trial, but she must've seen it coming. Because her entire defense was three words: God forgive you. She's probably stuck inside a leaky shelter, starving with no food and shivering with cold."

Jack sighs. He misses Serena and thinks of her quite often. Wondering when he will have the privilege of standing next to her again crushes his once unconquerable spirit.

If Jack is a lion, boldness and courage will follow in his wake. Every obstacle will be rushed at head-on. The football team will valiantly charge behind him like a pride. On the other hand, Toby is the cunning snake. His constant plots and apathetic slyness alienate him from Jack's group, and no one trusts him.

After a few more rounds of chess and checkers, the rain dissipates. The town begins to stir. People begin walking on the newly watered sidewalks. Mr. Stanton gives the word to open the diner once the people begin to populate the streets. Just after that, Stephanie comes to work wearing her uniform and a brown bandanna to tie her hair back out of her face.

The day continues. Jack and Lawrence rotate between taking orders and cleaning tables while Tomas takes his usual station cooking food on the stove. Mr. Stanton assembles the orders. Stephanie rotates between helping Mr. Stanton and filling and refilling drinks. After the final customers from the lunch rush have left, Toby and Mary, closely flanked by two of Toby's cronies, saunter in.

Everyone falls quiet. They silently stare to see what the four will do. Toby does not appear conscious of the silence. If anything, he relishes the attention the customers are unintentionally giving him. Jack notices Mary whisper something into Toby's ear. Toby shakes his head as if to veto Mary's idea and sidles over to Jack and Lawrence.

"Your salutes were late and sloppy," he declares.

All the gazes seem to press upon the two waiters. Neither of them speaks, but they steadily return his gaze. This only unnerves Toby, so he superiorly sticks out his chin at them.

"May I prescribe a day of exile so you may practice your salute?" Toby asks as Jack and Lawrence keep returning his stare, leveling him with stoic expressions.

At these words, Toby's henchmen seize the two waiters and march them away, still dressed in their uniforms and aprons. Mr. Stanton rounds the corner and begins reprimanding Toby.

"Yo, Toby. Why are yuh haulin' away ma workers?"

"Because they are insolent and deserve punishment." Toby sounds like a young Owl.

"Yuh might be a leader o' some upshot organization, but yuh a bad one," returns Mr. Stanton. He points at Jack and Lawrence. "This is why rebellions start. See, if'n some authority begins oppressin' people, every evil act is a reason to rebel against the authority."

"They wouldn't dare. I have authority, and I wield it too. If they did, they'd be crushed. Be gone old man." Toby walks smartly out of the diner with Mary.

Toby holds his head high, but Mary appears more apologetic. Their disappearance leaves the diner in a state of quiet tenseness. Mr. Stanton feels their absence, and an irritable mood descends upon him like a net upon a fish. Mr. Stanton mutters some words under his breath that would have definitely earned him a sentence in the forest beyond the river. He angrily reaches for the phone. He knows Josiah and Perceval have the day off, but with all the exiles Toby deals out, he needs his other employees on their day off. He knows they will be in bad moods, but he doesn't mind.

CHAPTER 18

# REUNIONS AND COLLABORATIONS

Toby's deputies drop Jack and Lawrence off at the opposite side of the river, and the two young men march into the forest to begin their day of exile. Lawrence's expression remains indifferent, and he starts rummaging through the underbrush around the river. Jack stares at his friend.

"Whatever it is you are looking for, it's not here!" Jack exclaims.

"No, it is here. A few days ago, I came here and hid a package of camping supplies and stuff. I thought I would get exiled one day, so I prepared for it," Lawrence explains as he hunts for the hidden contraband. "Lots of us have. It's kind of a way to have an excuse to go out into the forest. Break a rule on purpose so that Toby exiles you, and you will have the rest of the day in the forest. I just prepare for it."

"All right. I'll help you look. I'm following you."

"Great, Jack. Let's do this."

The pair scour the underbrush for Lawrence's emergency cache. But they cannot find it among the foliage.

"Are you sure you did not forget to take that cache out?" Jack asks.

"If I forgot, we're in serious trouble."

The pair keep searching. They find themselves traveling farther away from the bridge. By keeping the bridge somewhat in sight, getting lost is not an issue. Lawrence, who momentarily pauses from his work, glances upward and notices some smoke.

"Uh, Jack. I think I've found something you may want to see."

Jack hurries to Lawrence's position, striding over a thorn bush, and looks in the direction Lawrence is pointing. What Jack sees surprises him, a light gray column that twists and morphs into many different shapes as it spirals up beyond the trees and disappears into the bleak sky.

"That's definitely someone's camp," Jack says quietly.

Together, Jack and Lawrence eagerly race into the forest. The pair completely forget about searching for Lawrence's cache. They follow the wisp of smoke until they nearly fall to their deaths into a small canyon. At the bottom is a small camp. A crude moss-over-stick dwelling stands beside a small stream. In its center, some meat is cooking over a modest fire. If they had paid better attention, they would have noticed footprints by the bush they are using as cover.

A figure emerges from the caves on the other side of the canyon. The person appears small from their vantage point, wearing a once-white T-shirt and extremely dirty overalls. One of the straps has been torn free, and the figure is unrecognizable, caked in dirt. However, Jack notices a recognizable feature. His gaze remains fixated on the person's hair, which has within seconds of the discovery captivated him. It is rather short with blonde streaks and a puffed-out appearance.

He quietly calls out, "Serena?"

The individual starts and appears to scan the underbrush at the top of the canyon. Jack believes that whoever the person is, was startled by his sudden outburst. Lawrence looks moodily at Jack because of the stealthy nature of their mission and that Jack has foiled it. Jack stands up and tries to find a way down into the canyon. In his mind, the figure before him can be only one person.

Finally, Lawrence surrenders the element of stealth and carefully ventures after him.

As Jack approaches, Serena recognizes who the two guys are and begins to walk toward them. When Jack and Serena meet, their hands join like a pair of dancers. Serena stares into Jack's face.

"How did you find me?" Serena whispers. Her question proves to be rhetorical as she diverts her gaze from Jack's face to the medium-sized fire crackling merrily on canyon undergrowth. Lawrence is also looking contentedly at the flames.

Jack and Lawrence marvel at the design of the shelter as they fashion a pair of fishing rods from sticks. After the tour of her camp is complete, and they cast Serena's line into the stream, Serena starts a conversation while they wait for the fish to bite.

"How has Christville been doing since I left?"

"Perfectly awful!" Jack answers with an exasperated smile.

Lawrence nods in agreement.

Jack's smile turns sheepish as he kicks off the story. "The Owls have started an organization called the YMRP. It has been designed to provide relief for those who fell for your ..." He pauses as if searching for the right word.

"Trap," Lawrence finishes for him. He picks up Jack's melancholy tale. "It sounds like a decent idea except for a few minor reasons. First, Toby and your sister, Mary, have been selected to lead the entire project, and he hasn't accomplished anything except making Jack and members of his football team sign on and imposing insane rules upon its members."

Jack continues, "He's outlawed football, going into the woods, and having friends of the opposite gender. He's also making us salute him whenever we are in his presence. He's acting like a modern-day Haman. What's more, I could go on, but really, I think you get the idea."

Serena nods as if empathizing with their struggle. She strolls to the edge of the camp, where she stands, deep in thought. Jack's and Lawrence's gazes follow her as she thinks of the right words.

At length, Serena faces them. "Let me tell you something, Jack. You and Lawrence are right to not openly rebel against Toby. I, in a way, rebelled against society and now look at me. I am an exile and am not welcome in Christville until Anaeus is not angry with me anymore. I wish this was not the case, but breaking rules as protest against those rules is not a good idea."

Jack's eyes turn toward the ground and a smile alights upon his face. His confidence returns exponentially, armed with this reassurance from his protector. His eyes stray back to Serena's dirt-stained form. Before she can speak, Jack breaks the silence.

"Sorry. I'm wondering what this stuff is," Jack says, rubbing some of the soot that has collected on Serena between his fingers.

"What stuff?" Serena asks.

"The stuff that has absolutely covered you."

Confused, Serena glances at her watery reflection in the stream. A look of surprise flashes across her face as she recoils from the bubbling brook. "Whatever it is, I need a bath."

They spend the rest of the day exploring. Lawrence and Jack considerably miss this activity. The trio seems to brighten together, and they spend the night in jubilation. Even the bugs and humidity fail to curb their happiness. They make their beds on fresh pine boughs under a dark, starry sky. The fire senses the glee in its oxygen diet and cheerfully crackles throughout the night.

Instead of immediately sinking into sleep, Jack, Lawrence, and Serena continue to converse around the campfire. They laugh and tell numerous jokes and comical campfire stories until they arrive at the crux of their conversation. They try to discover a route to release Serena from her green prison. Cloaked in the starry darkness, the trio plot Serena's escape.

"I studied Christville's history, and the governing body often states how long the exile is to last while the accused can still hear it," Lawrence says.

"Except the Owls deliberately never stated how long I was to stay an exile. I hope I'm not out here for too much longer. Or at least I hope my parents start protesting," Serena says.

"So, you're saying that if we can get Anaeus to specifically say how long your sentence should have been, you could free yourself by simply waiting," Lawrence exclaims.

"Precisely." Serena smiles. She knows that this idea of getting out of exile sounds simple, but it isn't. "I'm not beating the Owls in the traditional sense where I fight them to win. I'll wait out the rest of my time. Then, just act as if nothing has happened. Let's see Anaeus when I do the same old adventures like last summer."

Jack and Lawrence look at each other and silently nod their approval.

"Well now, if that's all we have to do, let's try to get some sleep." Lawrence yawns.

Sleep comes quickly for Jack. However, a nightmare haunts him. He dreams that he, his brothers, and all his friends convene for a normal game of football. Despite his attempts, an inexplicable force keeps him from participating. The game starts. James runs for one touchdown, Lawrence catches nine passes, including another touchdown, Tomas plays hard as a cornerback, and Perceval completes three touchdown passes. However, as the game ends, the Owls, Toby, and Mary appear on the field and issue denouncements, punishments, and warnings, accusing everyone at once. Toby's gestapo moves like the Flash, quickly and efficiently apprehending one player after another. One by one, Jack's friends turn and fade into oblivion until he is the only person left on the field, facing the cheat Toby, his enforcers, and Anaeus, the man who planned Serena's false denouncement and exile.

Suddenly, the vision blurs, and he finds himself running in a forest, trying to go back to the city, but the forest seems determined to pull him deeper into the foliage. He fights his way on hands and knees until breaking through becomes impossible. He feels as if he is being swallowed by green as all manner of plants press around him.

Jack wakes up in a cold sweat. His senses blur. Light pours over the camp where he was sleeping. The sun arrives too early, deciding to make an appearance today, and the world greets its warmth. Stumbling out of the camp, groggy and aching, Jack strolls to the modest remade fire that blazes cheerfully underneath three juicy pieces of cooking fish. What type of fish it is, he cannot tell.

Jack plunges his hands into the stream. The watery cold swirls around his hands. Pressing them to his face obliterates any vestiges of drowsiness. Jack leads a short prayer, and breakfast is served.

After breakfast, Serena accompanies them to the bridge that crosses the river. The trio chat until they overhear the sound of cracking branches. Serena vanishes into the forest and observes from the dark shadows. When Serena vanishes, Toby's men lumber into view. Jack and Lawrence are relieved to see that neither Toby nor Mary decided to accompany their enforcers. Jack and Lawrence march boldly across the rickety structure spanning the river. They all march back to Christville in silence.

## CHAPTER 19

# A MOTHER'S LOVE AND PUBLIC SECRETS

Jack returns to his house, where he takes a long nap. After his nap, Jack goes over to Serena's house. He wants to tell Annemarie and Sheldon about Serena's condition. He strides up to the white screen door and bangs on it three times. Sheldon answers the door.

"Yes, can I help you?"

"Good morning, Pastor Sheldon. I came to share how Serena has been doing for the past couple of weeks," Jack says.

Sheldon looks around outside and then at Jack. "Come in." His voice is almost a whisper.

Jack rarely speaks to Sheldon and does not think of him as a man with many words to accompany him. Sheldon leads Jack to their spacious living room.

"Have a seat. I'll be with you in a moment."

Jack calmly seats himself. Presently, Annemarie and Sheldon greet him. The door slides shut after the pair enter. Jack alights upon the edge of the straight-backed chair, not wanting to fall asleep in the middle of his report. Sheldon sits opposite him on the couch, while Annemarie takes up her place on the rocking chair.

Jack slowly draws a deep breath and begins, "When I was in exile, I found Serena."

Annemarie's and Sheldon's eyes widen as if this is news they want to hear after all.

Feeling unsure, Jack continues, "D-D-Don't get me wrong. She's doing fine. Although, uh, she doesn't have a lot of food to choose from." He omits the fact that Serena has become quite dirty, but he describes how he found her and what they had done yesterday.

Annemarie eagerly reacts. "I must go see her as soon as I can. I know the exact location Jack is describing. It was where my old hideout was located when I was younger."

Jack raises one eyebrow in confusion.

Instead of matching his wife's eagerness, Sheldon expresses concern for his wife and advises caution. "It is enough that Serena is exiled, but for you to waste what you have reconstructed over the past years would be too much for me."

"Surveillance is terrible outside of town. Besides, who would miss me if I disappeared for two hours tomorrow? I have nothing tomorrow anyway except to argue with Leah and Mariah or whoever else happens to be at the ladies' society." Annemarie scoffs animatedly.

"I can't stop you, but remember," Sheldon lowers his voice, "I don't want you to cause trouble."

Jack knows that, to this day, nobody allows Annemarie to forget the moment she went after Anaeus.

But Sheldon gives Annemarie his blessing. "Go and see Serena, but be careful. Our daughter is gone, and I don't want the same fate to befall you."

Annemarie nods her response and returns to thinking. Jack stands up and prepares to leave, having concluded his business with the Rogers. When he steps outside the living room, he accidentally hits Mary's face with the door. Mary recoils in a panic, rubbing her jaw, and scurries away like a frightened mouse. However, Jack is not excessively concerned by Mary. But if he had dedicated an inkling amount of time to scan the floor before he left, he might have discovered a smooth glass near the door.

Meanwhile, Mary hurries into the peaceful garden to process the information she had gathered from her parents' conversation. Her mouth still hurts from an unsuspecting Jack hitting her with the door. As Mary mulls over what she just heard, Toby strolls into the garden. His figure is hidden by a dark trench coat equipped with a loose hood. If he were wielding a crooked sickle, he would undoubtedly pass as the grim reaper.

Mary rises from her chair in the garden and looks into his almond-shaped eyes. She recalls how well their friendship has fared over the past ten months. Toby might be a cheat, but since he has friends now, it appears as though he might move on from his past.

"Hi, Toby. I was not expecting you," Mary greets him.

"I needed a walk."

"Oh, well, is there anything we can talk about?"

"Not much. Any news?"

"I got some news about Serena."

"Oh, well, let's hear it."

"Well, it appears Serena has been busy since the hearing. She lives off the land quite easily in a small canyon about a twenty-minute walk north from the river." Mary tries to sound smug.

"Who did you eavesdrop on this time?"

"A conversation between Jack and my parents. Jack came over about thirty minutes ago and reported everything to my parents. I listened in."

"Ah, that explains it. Jack and Lawrence should be out and about. I exiled them yesterday."

"Yes, and everyone else in town knows."

"I don't really care about that. I'm enjoying my position, and I'll rise through the ranks and become an Owl. That will be great."

"Now, that's great for you, but enough of the far future. Do you have any plans for today?"

"Not much, but I am expected at the church soon, so I should probably head that way. I will see you soon."

Toby promptly exits the garden. As soon as he disappears, Mary returns to her seat. She mulls over the conversation. Was all that information really worth sharing with Toby? Perhaps not, but hopefully nothing will come of it.

After a few minutes, Mary rises and exits the garden and steps out onto the sidewalk. She has no real destination in mind. She finds herself at the church. She walks inside and heads toward the basement. She hears some indistinct mumbling behind a closed door. She stops to listen, gently placing her ear to the door.

"Once that is done, I want Jack to take the blame for this. I can accomplish this using the information that Mary has so graciously given me too."

Mary pushes away from the door and scampers away and out of the church. She discards every positive thought about Toby. She had most definitely surrendered the wrong information. Now Toby is plotting against Serena. Despite their bad relationship, Mary does want the best for Serena. She knows Toby must be stopped. She had wanted Serena to join regular society so she would not be targeted like she is now in the first place.

## CHAPTER 20

# MISINFORMATION AND IGNORANCE

Jack had returned to Christville with an optimistic attitude, dethroning his depression. When he returns to his job at the diner, Mr. Stanton surprises him with a dish of French fries at their lunch break. After the lunch rush ends, the workers begin preparations for dinner. They have started to clean the tables of any and all visible debris when Anaeus strides into the restaurant.

If Mr. Stanton has any grudges against Anaeus for Toby dragging his employees away to the forest yesterday, even Sherlock Holmes would not notice. Mr. Stanton approaches Anaeus in a mild manner and collects his order. While Jack prepares the food, he tries to think of how to extract the words required from Anaeus. Lawrence comically waves his hand over Jack's eyes to bring him back to reality. Since Anaeus is the only customer in the diner, the order is assembled. Jack is elected to take it out to Anaeus.

Jack approaches the table and hands Anaeus his order. He has just turned around when Anaeus barks, "Are you Jack Irving?"

"Yeah, what of it?" replies Jack taken aback.

"Toby said you were being rude to him. What do you have to say?"

"When was this?" Jack asks, attempting to sound humble.

"Ten o'clock this morning if you want the time," Anaeus growls, his voice boiling over with concealed wrath.

"I was working at ten o'clock this morning, and I never saw him. You must be looking for someone else," Jack says, trying in vain to diffuse Anaeus's amassing anger, or at least deflect it toward someone else.

Anaeus remains undeterred. "If I hear that you've been rude to the person I placed in a position of power, then you could find yourself with more exile than Toby could give you."

Jack nods. This exchange with Anaeus has assured him that his mission is doomed to fail. Better to address him once his unpredictable mood changes. His plan requires a thorough overhaul and another opportunity when Anaeus's temper is more diffusible. Jack escapes back to the kitchen, where Mr. Stanton throws his arm over his shoulder.

"There wasn't much yuh cud do," Mr. Stanton comforted him.

Jack nods, and work proceeds as usual.

After work, Jack strides home, ready to unwind and change from his usual work attire. He relaxes on his bed, allowing the aches in his feet to recede. After an hour, he goes for a walk. As he leaves his house, he sees Toby and Mary strolling by. Jack notices that Toby's enforcers do not accompany Toby, so he decides to follow them at a safe distance. *What are they thinking*, he wonders. The road they leisurely meander down sharply slopes down to the forest on their left. There are no houses on this side of the road. As they travel, Jack spots Perceval waiting at the woodland's edge. Upon seeing Toby, Perceval dives into the glen. Toby watches this as well. Shouting some indecipherable order, Toby hesitates and then reluctantly plunges into the shade of the woods. Mary follows, and then Jack eagerly rushes into the forest.

Toby and Mary move slowly as they labor through the undergrowth. They carefully navigate around every obstacle. To Jack, it appears as if Perceval wants them to follow him. Jack watches as Perceval waits for them to clear a hazard in their path before moving through the next.

At first, Jack tries not to be noticed. However, during the trek, Toby looks behind him and sees him. Jack does not want to cause trouble, so he raises his hand and shouts, "I'm with you."

Toby says nothing and presses forward. At length, Perceval begins to hasten. Toby and Mary quicken their pace as well. However, Jack does not find it difficult to keep up. Then Perceval emerges into a clearing. He strolls to the center, turns around, and faces Toby. Jack decides to watch from his vantage point at the forest's edge.

Toby stops and shouts, "You have broken the rules, Perceval."

"Well, who's going to hold me accountable?" Perceval replies.

"Me, because I am your leader, and you will follow my rules."

"No, I won't," Perceval says with defiance.

Toby growls in response, but Perceval remains silent. He snaps his fingers, and from the outskirts of the forest, Jack sees his team rallying to rebel against Toby, who is without his bodyguards and only has Mary at his side. Toby is wide-eyed as all his followers gather around Perceval.

"All right, guys, let's finish him," Perceval declares.

His followers advance toward Toby.

"Wait! Jack, I thought you were with me," Toby shouts in desperation.

Meanwhile, Jack emerges from the forest. His smile is broad, and he chuckles. Toby, in the other hand, is noticeably scared.

"No, Toby. I was just saying that so you would not get mad at me," Jack replies.

Toby gasps and turns toward the mob of his followers closing around him and Mary, who looks petrified into silence. Suddenly, Toby pushes Mary into the crowd of teenagers. Mary shrieks more from surprise than fear as they rush upon her. Toby runs toward the forest. But the members of Jack's football team are faster and stronger than him. The chase is over quickly. Arthur and Tomas tackle him from behind. Meanwhile, Perceval helps Mary to her feet and walks her over to where Toby lies on the ground. Then Jack, deciding this scene has lasted long enough, brings his demand to Perceval.

"No, Perceval. You will not hurt Mary. She did nothing against you."

Perceval pauses and looks at Jack. Jack knows he does not want to mistreat Mary but rather to dominate Toby at this point.

Releasing Mary, Perceval turns to her and says, "Go home, Mary. Our business is with Toby."

Mary runs away as fast her dress will allow her. Jack and his football team gather around the toppled leader of the YMRP.

"Since you are the leader of this revolution, Perceval, you pronounce judgement," Jack declares.

Perceval beams. He has waited for the day when he can take charge of something. Yet he hesitates, as he is not prepared to decide what Toby's punishment will be for mistreating him and the other members of the YMRP. After some standing around, Perceval is ready to speak.

"I say we dunk him in the swimming hole!" shouts someone from the crowd.

The others cheer their approval. Toby is hoisted up by ten strong young men. Two hold his hands in front of him, and they begin to carry him toward the swimming hole. As the reality of Toby's situation sinks into his mind, he transforms into a writhing, struggling, screaming demon. But Jack's team is too strong. Toby can't break free.

Standing on the bank of the swimming hole, James and Perceval take Toby's arms, while Tomas and Jerome grab his legs and another player named Ulysses pushes from behind, leaning into Toby's side.

"One, two, three!" the group chants loudly as Perceval, James, Tomas, Jerome, and Ulysses swing Toby to the shouted rhythm and hurl Toby into the middle of the deep end.

However, Toby manages to grab James and both fall into the water making a tremendous *splash*!

Toby and James immediately surface. Toby spits, sputters, and thrashes to keep himself afloat, while James wipes his eyes and begins to make his way to the bank. Toby suddenly lunges at James, wrapping his arms around his neck. James lets out a choking grunt. Despite his best efforts, he begins to sink under Toby's weight.

John and Jerome jump into the swimming hole to help their brother. The water is deep, and both are forced to tread water to stay afloat. John begins by breaking Toby's grip on James's neck. His work is enough for James to get some air. James lashes out at Toby, pushing him off. Then Jack leaps into the shallow end. The quartet haul Toby into the shallow end and dunk him under the water. Toby lies flat on the water, buoying him up, allowing him to draw a deep breath. However, James places a hand on his face and forces it beneath the swirling surface. After a few seconds, Jack and his brothers allow Toby up. The four brothers scatter to the edge of the swimming hole before Toby can lunge at them.

However, as a furious Toby attempts to climb out of the swimming hole, Josiah pushes him back into the water. Toby angrily flings water at him. But the others dip their hands into the swimming hole to fling water at him. Dejected, Toby exits the swimming hole and navigates through the mass surrounding its bank. He runs home soaked, embarrassed, and angry. He is also filled with a sweet feeling of revenge.

"I will have revenge, Jack. Let's see how you respond when I have your precious Serena wrapped in my arms instead of yours," Toby seethes. Although the day is warm, the dampness feels frigid when exposed to the breeze. But Toby's anger burns warm and heats his body against the cold.

As he walks, he spots Perceval's protector, Sarah, wandering in the forest. Toby's eyes widen, as he knows how he will punish Perceval for his betrayal and rebellion. He assumes Sarah is walking home. He waits at a bend in the path. As Sarah rounds the bend, Toby leaps into her way, pushing her to the ground.

"Good evening, Sarah," Toby says maliciously.

Sarah's eyes widen as Toby pounces on her, pressing her into the forest floor.

CHAPTER 21

# TO FACE A FEAR

The following day smiles upon Christville, but the humidity hangs like a heavy blanket, transforming the oxygen into a thick soup.

Mary awakes early because of the incessant humidity. She slams her window shut and wanders downstairs for breakfast. After finishing her meal, she returns to her room to read a book. The air-conditioning kicks in, and the atmosphere inside the house contrasts the wretched, humid weather outside. She is thankful for the relief.

Annemarie walks to Mary's room and stands in the doorway.

"I am leaving for the women's meeting, and I was wondering if you would like to come. I know the conversation can be boring, but I think a few of your friends will be there."

"Sure. I might not stay the entire time though."

Mary descends the stairs, and the two depart to the ladies' group. Mary hears the screen door slam behind them.

The humidity hits them like a wall as they stroll throughout the town. Annemarie tries to make good time by quickening her pace, but Mary lags behind because of the heat. In response, Annemarie slows down, and the pair silently make their way to the church. They arrive early. Some members are present, including three of Mary's friends, who already braved the intense humidity.

The meeting starts, and the conversation does not offer anything to be enthused over. Mary and her friends sit at their own table and begin to chat. Their conversation casually meanders down the weather lane, across hilarious story street, visits the family business store, and halts because the meeting is over for lunchtime.

After lunch, Mary returns to her room to resume reading for a while. The sun lazily begins to sink into the horizon.

Late in the afternoon, Mary begins to close the curtains. But next door, she spies a suspicious dark trench coat sneaking into the forest. A sinking feeling of dread enters her mind. *There is no time. Serena must be warned as soon as possible. But to go into the forest, that is unacceptable. What if someone finds out? That does not matter now.*

Mary leaves the comfort of the house, plunges into the humid air, and cautiously enters the forest. It is slightly cooler under the shade, but the bugs torment her. The shadows lengthen, and the forest feels darker. Mary fearfully follows the dirt trail. She feels the trees sneer at her from above. The humidity attempts to stop her. Her mind wants her to retreat to her bed and the air-conditioning. But she plods along, alert to every sound in the forest. At the clearing, Mary halts to scan the grass. Locating the no trespassing sign, she walks down the path toward the river to the north.

Soon she stands on the bridge, but she does not cross. Instead, she stands there.

She hears voices in the distance, and her muscles tense in fear. The rumble steadily crescendos and splits into two separate voices, and they seem to be having an intense conversation as they expertly pick their way through the foliage. Although Mary wants to run into the forest, her feet do not obey. But she need not have worried, because out of the forest comes Jack and Lawrence. Mary commands herself to relax and orders her fears to cease.

"Mary, what brings you out here?" asks a surprised Jack.

"I need to see Serena. I have to warn her!"

"Warn her? About what?" Lawrence asks.

"I believe Toby is going to attack Serena tonight. I saw him going into the woods about a half hour ago. I overheard that he was planning to do it previously, but he needed to find exactly where Serena was located." Mary does not mention that she had leaked the information.

Jack pauses the conversation as his mind digests the situation. But the apprehension developing within the conversation compels Mary to speak again.

"We need to find Serena now! Toby has the location, and he might be there now."

Jack cuts her off. "You think Toby is going to try to take my girl, that he is somewhere in the forest right now, and he knows exactly where he's going?"

"Right," Mary says.

"We have no time to waste. Even if this is a hoax, Serena should know."

The trio make it to Serena's camp in record time.

CHAPTER 22

# THE REPORT AND
# THE REASSIGNMENT

Earlier in the day, Jack, and Lawrence start their own trek through the forest. They know it will take around ten minutes. They have memorized the way there. Jack clasps his large thermos of ice water. But they are still hampered by the dense terrain. The sky above wears her traditional gray dress, and rain threatens to dump her wet glitter should anyone curse her choice of clothes today. Humidity causes sticky skin and makes the heat oppressive. Darkness and shadow populate the area like the people of a city. Despite this, Jack and Lawrence reach the canyon without much difficulty.

Serena expects Jack and Lawrence as much as the shepherds outside Bethlehem foresaw the angel. Her daily routine is finished. Her hair is damp from the swim she has taken recently. She reclines in the shade with a smooth rock at her back. Jack waves to Serena from the top of the canyon. She has not stirred a muscle except to swat away the annoying bugs for several minutes, but she rises upon noticing the pair as Jack and Lawrence laboriously descend the canyon rocky walls.

If she had been more attentive, she might have caught a faint glimpse of a phantom person spying on them from the top of the canyon wall. He lies flat on his belly, wearing a dark coat for camouflage. Sweat streams into his stinging eyes, but he does not take notice of it. The forest's shade practically turns Toby invisible. He clutches a jagged rock in his hands, and his catlike eyes play about Jack, Lawrence, and Serena. To Toby, this is better than he had hoped. Now, he can step forward as an eye-witness. He can say Serena seduced Jack and Lawrence. Toby can easily blame his crime on Jack and Lawrence and exile them forever. He finds his plan very simple.

"I love it when pieces fall into place by themselves. Now I will play this game again."

Toby smiles maliciously. He can barely contain his excitement. However, he crouches like a lion waiting to pounce on his prey. Only one obstacle can interfere with his plan. Jack and Lawrence must conclude their conversation and leave. When they eventually leave, he will strike quick and hard. He will satisfy his thirst for revenge on Jack and permanently secure his power at the same time.

"First, Serena, then Jack and Lawrence, then domination. Finally, my plan is secure. If I keep to it, many glorious rewards will follow. Wait Jack said my name."

"It was pretty serious. You don't try to drown someone. I get it Toby is mad, but he should have been more gracious as a leader. Honestly, I let my anger get the best of me because James is my brother. So yeah, me and my brothers jumped on Toby and dunked him in the shallows." Jack retells.

"Well, it was nice to see Perceval lead his own rebellion. He had a plan and executed it." Responds Lawrence.

"Well, yes, but the bad news is that I got the opportunity to talk to Anaeus, and he accused me of harassing Toby, and he really seemed to think I was guilty. I'm not going to ask Anaeus if he's just going to accuse me of stuff."

This frustrates Serena's plans. She knew she would be waiting to be released from this prison to learn that her former ploy has failed slightly aggravates her, "I did not think he would do that Jack. However, my idea was rather sneaky. Anaeus always hated it when I tried to sneak around him. I should have known that. Next time you see him, just ask him when my exile will end."

"But that's so simple."

"That's what makes it good. Better yet, he can't just exile you without arousing suspicion."

"OK, I'll try it tomorrow."

As the sun, weary of its conquest, decides to rest and let night take over, Jack and Lawrence, after saying their goodbyes, return home for the night. Serena strolls to her camp to settle down and count some sheep. Suddenly, her vision blurs and turns black.

CHAPTER 23

# DELIVERANCE

Serena groggily awakens to find her hands bound above her head to a hanging branch, which is pulled down by her weight. She realizes she is only wearing her swimsuit. Her bare feet barely touch the ground, and her head throbs from the resounding blow. Through her blurry vision, her gaze erratically happens upon a dark figure hunched over her fire. The hood on his coat obscures his face.

"Who are you?" Serena asks, trying to sound imperious and failing.

"Don't be so fake. Hasn't anyone ever taught you to speak only when spoken to?" the mysterious individual retorts.

The individual's voice sounds eerily familiar. Then Serena remembers it from her trial. It's as if a lightning bolt rocks through her brain. After all, more words had left his lips than any other person's.

"I don't need any more clues. I know you, Toby. But what are you doing here?" Serena asks, although she knows the answer. Her fingers toy with the rope, vainly seeking a weakness in the knots that hold her fast to the tree.

"Because you're mine now." Toby throws back his hood and glares at her.

At these words, Serena's eyes widen. She violently throws herself at Toby, straining against the ropes that hold her. But the ropes are well tied. She needs something to help free herself, but she might as well relocate to Mount Everest.

Toby watches with amusement, as if Serena is an entertaining stage performer. This enrages her even more, and she flings herself forward, vainly attempting to break the cords. Finally, she stops thrashing and limply hangs from the tree. Toby takes this opportunity to approach cautiously. He reaches out his hand. But before he can touch her tanned body, Serena kicks him in the stomach. Toby staggers backward and painfully falls to one knee. The pain contorts his face into a hideous grimace.

"Did I say that you could touch me?" Serena shouts angrily.

"It is pointless to resist me. Give up and save yourself the hardship. I going to touch you one way or another." Toby coos, picking himself off the ground and massaging his chest where her foot connected.

Serena mentally withdraws to reflect on this. Toby holds every conceivable advantage. She has nowhere to run or fight. She is alone with someone who wants to do serious harm to her. She will tire herself out, and Toby will strike. It will soon be over. As if on cue, she feels the strength draining from her body like water down a drain. But if Toby desires her, he will have to pay a hefty price for her.

As she emerges from the emergency meeting within her mind, Serena notices Toby has disappeared. Confused, she scans the scene. Suddenly she feels a massive force slam into her side. Knuckles pierce deep below her ribcage. Her voice wears itself out screaming uncontrollably as the most intense pain she's ever experienced courses through her body. Then another fist slams into her from the other side in the exact same spot. She grits her teeth as a thousand lightning bolts race through her. Her vocal cords have run out of energy, and she hangs limp from the tree, breathing hard.

Toby reappears from behind her. "I got tired of waiting. Now, will you submit, or will I have to do more?"

Serena glares back at her attacker, showing she is not done yet. Toby prepares another punch, but instead of going for the face as Serena expects, he launches into an uppercut to her gut. If the ropes were not restraining her, she would have doubled over. Instead, she painfully lurches backward. Her wind is knocked out of her. Serena grimaces and moans in pain.

"I expect your answer. Your silence will be treated as refusal, and I intend to have your agreement even if we have to keep doing this all night."

Sluggishly and with painful effort, Serena staggers upright and hangs from the ropes. She regains her breath and promptly spits, "You will have to kill me first."

"You are stubborn. But that will not save you. Why don't you just give in? It will ease your suffering," Toby says. "Please consider my requests, and you would be free to go. I will leave after I have what I want. Nobody would need to know."

"But, I would be a shell of myself, filled with painful memories of what you did." Serena grimaces. Like a wounded animal, her strength is whittled down, but she is still dangerous and desperate. She grits her teeth in pain. Her head burns where Toby knocked her out, and she gasps for air.

Toby's smile vanishes and is replaced by another menacing scowl. "I see you need more convincing." He trudges over to the staff that lies neglected on the ground. Serena braces herself for the inevitable impact. Except a ray of the setting sun reflects off a knife blade. Although faint, Serena immediately notices the knife. Toby spots it too.

"Well, that's a relief. Now I don't need your submission." Toby scoffs as he retrieves the blade.

Serena grits her teeth in astonished horror. Her situation has gone from bad to tremendously worse. Toby strides toward her, knife in hand. He raises his other hand to block any blow Serena might throw. Serena glares defiantly back at him, waiting for him to get within range for another kick. She lashes out, but Toby dodges and, with his free hand, pins her bare leg to one side. He grabs one of the fastenings on the swimsuit and readies the knife to bite through the elastic fabric.

Serena squirms, trying to force Toby to let go of her swimsuit and get into position to strike again. But Toby hangs on tight to the fastening, and she can't get a kick in. Serena feels as if she has exhausted every trick and played every card. Toby has gotten to where she can't reach him. It would require a miracle for her to escape.

Just then, Mary, Jack, and Lawrence burst onto the scene.

"Toby! You get away from my girl! Now!" Jack yells. His fists clench, ready to fight.

Mary, on the other hand, hides her face, not wanting to witness what Jack and Lawrence will do to Toby for attempting to violate her older sister.

"Why do you think you can stop me?" Toby retorts scornfully.

"What makes you think we won't beat you till your face needs plastic surgery to look human again?" Lawrence snarls, returning his contemptuous glare. He seems excited to make good on his threat.

The trio advance into the campsite, but they stop, eyeing the knife in Toby's hand. Caught by surprise, Toby does not notice that he moved in front of Serena, who is mustering the strength for one final attack. She gathers the final few portions of energy remaining and aims a great kick at Toby.

Toby never sees what Serena is attempting, and he cannot react quickly enough. The shock from the blow sends Toby staggering backward. The knife flies out of his outstretched hand and falls at Mary's feet. He fails to regain his balance and erratically stumbles before violently collapsing. Toby's head bashes against a sharp rock, and lies motionless.

Serena hangs limply where she is tied. Shock prevails. Her breathing feels ragged and yet, it is all she can do. Feeling her friends approaching her, Serena mercifully blacks out again.

CHAPTER 24

# HOMECOMING AND RECONCILIATION

Serena and Mary sit in silence on the porch. An unnatural midevening turns cold around them. They draw their thin blankets tightly around themselves as they calmly sip lemonade.

Serena had replaced her swimsuit for a knee-length white dress with three pale doves sewn onto the front. She also had a hot bath. The dirt that littered her body is now cleansed. Dr. Irving was also contacted to look for any damage. He pronounced she has suffered no permanent injury.

Serena already believes that her physical wounds will bruise but in time will heal. However, the blow to her head will remain permanently enshrined upon the upper left side of her forehead. Dr. Irving applied a bandage around Serena's head and prescribed an antibiotic to terminate any possible infection.

Annemarie and Sheldon left after Serena related the entire tale from her exile to the point when Jack, Lawrence, and Mary had shown up to rescue her from Toby. She omits any part of Toby's assaulting her. She blames her injuries on a fall.

"How did you know to come?" Serena asks her sister.

"I eavesdropped on Toby, just like I do on everybody, I know. I tried to get Toby to you so I could dishonor him. It worked," Mary begins to relate the sorrowful tale.

"You see, Toby came to me at the summer party. I followed him after Anaeus yelled at you. I knew of his terrible reputation, but I decided to give him a chance. I saw a boy who needed friendship. From what you've told me, Anaeus must have found out about our friendship and ordered us to denounce you on a false charge. Looking back, I should not have participated in denouncing you. I just wanted to humiliate you. I went way too far. I regretted having to testify against you, but I had gone too far, and I had to follow through."

Mary's voice drips with sadness and regret as she speaks. Twice she is forced to stop and drink some lemonade. Tears stain her blanket, but she continues with her story.

"When the YMRP was formed, I continued my friendship with him. He was not a good leader, but he was a decent friend. I thought he had a change of heart, but I was wrong. I overheard him talking about what he was going to do to you. I should have gone to Jack earlier, but I could not find him. Then I caught up with Jack's group, but they were after Toby and let me go. The next day, I saw Toby go out into the forest and I just knew I had to warn you. Then I found Jack, and we went back. That's when we found you and, well ... that's it. I have given you a tale of my worst decisions."

As Mary ends her dreary tale, she drains her glass in one swallow and sits in quiet regret.

Serena replies, "Mary, I'm not calling your decisions good, but that was the bravest thing a person could have ever done."

"You think so?" Mary sniffs.

"Of course, because if you hadn't made friends with Toby, I would still be in exile with my arms bound above my head and Toby still driving away at me or worse. He would have been the one to return from the forest, accomplishing what he set out to do. All his plans would have succeeded, and I would become a victim," Serena says. "You may regret it, but God will honor you for it."

"Do you think so?"

"I believe so."

Neither speaks for a while. Then Mary, who has managed to recover most of her composure, states, "Let's be friends, and I am sorry for being a pain."

"Think nothing of it. I forgive you."

The two sisters sit alone on the porch until sleep nearly overcomes them. Then they march to bed.

When Serena shuts the parlor door, the bronze owl topples from its stand again, but this time, its wings break and it remains on the floor for the night.

The next day, the YMRP is disbanded. This news is met with joy from its members and horror from Anaeus. Serena's plan has worked to perfection, even though the emotional wounds Toby inflicted will accompany her for life.

CHAPTER 25

# THE STAGE IS SET

Word of Serena's bizarre return to Christville spreads faster than a wildfire fanned by the Santa Anna winds. The utter dissolution of YMRP and Toby's mysterious disappearance creates a countercultural mystery that downright befuddles every resident.

The Owls instantly learn of her reappearance. However, they encounter an undeniable problem: Toby has vanished. Toby's baffling departure is a serious problem for Anaeus. He calls a meeting in the church sanctuary to discuss the issue.

Anaeus opens the conversation. "Since Toby has disappeared, we will need someone to accuse Serena again. I move that we ask the widow Mrs. Lars."

"No, Anaeus. No. Mrs. Lars might be a zealous believer, but let her be innocent of this," Oceanus demands.

"Well then, Oceanus, if not her, then who?"

"You shall bring the charges against Serena. You are behind her exile. You should bring her to court" Titus declares.

The hall becomes silent, and every Owl looks toward Titus. Titus looks ahead as if daring anyone to challenge his idea.

"But I'm an Owl. I should be exempt of discourse with other people. It would be too hard," Anaeus exclaims. He wants to get someone else to bring his grievances against Serena.

"You think this is difficult, Anaeus. It is a simple matter to me. You are an Owl. One of the smartest, most influential persons in this town. Your intellect should be substantial enough to silence any rebellion from Serena. If she is guilty of a specific sin, then it should be easy. You will be able to expose that," Titus explains. He turns to the other Owls. "Is everyone agreed?"

The other Owls nod thoughtfully. Their approval prompts Titus's attention to turn back to Anaeus, who feels defeated and isolated.

"It is settled now. If she has committed a specific sin, you will bring charges against Serena," Titus declares.

"Do I still have your blessing?" Anaeus doubts if he still retains the Owls' support.

"Don't make a fool of yourself, Anaeus," Titus replies.

The meeting is ended.

*Not quite according to plan, but my plan can work. It must*, thinks Anaeus as he exits the sanctuary. His thoughts are interrupted when he knocks over a surprised Josiah. Josiah is acting as if he is vacuuming the foyer and wanting to proceed to the worship sanctuary. Anaeus helps the adolescent to his feet. The pair exchange brief smiles and walk away.

Meanwhile, Josiah has overheard every word in the meeting. The Owls are imperious. To ask one of them to speak quietly is like asking them to defend themselves on false charges. After Anaeus leaves the church, Josiah races out the back door of the church thinking, *Serena must know this*. He reaches the football field, where Jack has just started a game of tag. Josiah arrives gasping and panting for breath. Tomas meets Josiah at the edge of the field.

"Better walk around a mite. Yuh look yuh just ran a marathon without any training."

"Serena must know about this. It's urgent." Josiah pants.

"And what should Serena know? Speak up, and take some water too." Tomas leads the way over to the edge of the game.

"The Owls plan to denounce Serena again. However, Anaeus is

going to accuse Serena himself. I think he'll use the same arguments as last time," Josiah explains between alternated deep breaths and gulps of water from a canteen Tomas handed him. He scans the crowd but cannot see Serena's face in the enthusiastic crowd. "Do you know where Serena is?"

Now it is Tomas's turn to scan the crowd. "No. I don't see her. Let's tell Jack. He'll make sure the information gets to Serena."

They search for Jack. The game of tag is using a large area to accommodate the large number of participants of all ages, from small eight-year-olds to many of Jack's football team members, who are in high school. Many older girls who are affiliated with the football team are also present. Josiah sees Perceval breathing hard and watching the center of the field. He and Tomas search the faces.

"There's Jack!" Tomas exclaims. "On the other side of the field near the forty-yard line."

They slip and weave their way through the game. Josiah regains some of his energy, so he can keep up with Tomas. They reach Jack quite quickly. He is standing around, scanning downfield. Serena is standing nearby. Stephanie and Sarah stand beside Serena.

"Jack, Josiah has something to say," Tomas says.

Jack and Serena peer in their direction. Serena says nothing, but Jack speaks up.

"Hey, Tomas, Josiah. What can I do for you?"

"I overheard something that you and Serena will want to hear."

"OK. What is it?" Jack asks.

"Anaeus is going to lead a trial against Serena. The Owls are forcing him to do it himself. It is quite possible that the Owls don't like him," Josiah reports.

Jack and Serena look at each other. Nobody speaks, but it appears that Jack and Serena are conversing about Josiah's news.

The silence grows too awkward for Josiah, who says, "Since that's everything I have to say, I going to go now. See you soon, Jack."

"Yes, see you," Jack replies.

Josiah nods and walks away. Tomas also leaves but without saying anything.

"Do you think you can win this time?" Jack asks Serena.

"It is very possible. The Owls can hide their compliance with Anaeus by ruling against him, which means allowing me to go free. One thing is obvious: Anaeus's list of allies is growing thin. Besides, now that Anaeus himself is challenging me, my knowledge about the past trial will make more sense to other people."

Jack nods, and the pair rejoin the game.

## CHAPTER 26

# THE FINAL BATTLE

Serena does not sleep the night before the trial. Either she will obliterate her grandfather in front of the entire congregation or she will still be guilty. But Anaeus controls the jury.

"What a trap!" Serena whispers to herself, frustrated and yanking the light sheet over herself.

After rolling over for what seems like the eighty-fifth time, she finally falls asleep. She awakens from the depths of slumber to the clattering sound of dishes downstairs.

Serena is brimming over with nervous energy like a boiling pot of potatoes on the stove. She can barely keep from fidgeting during the church service. *Can I really beat Anaeus? Is there any way for me to be innocent?*

Sure enough, as Josiah had detailed yesterday, Anaeus accuses her and proposes bringing her back to trial. Serena calms and mentally rallies herself. She will fight and beat the charges.

That afternoon, Serena sits pensively in the defendant box for the second time in a month, wearing another T-shirt and pair of overalls. She masks her emotions behind a wall of seriousness and tries to keep her eyes in a near closed state.

Anaeus strolls up to the defendant box and opens a private

conversation. "Serena, do you know why you were exiled?" he asks. His voice is calm and insightful.

"Because, according to you, I'm a rebellious girl who won't submit to the normal role of women in this town," Serena says nonchalantly to the point of being disrespectful.

"Correct, and I presume you know what will happen today?"

"I might get exiled again." Serena sighs as if she would like to answer the question in a different way, but she knows Anaeus would rebuke her preferred answer.

"Yes. In your state, you will. You are a rebellious girl, but you can also be reasoned with. Hear me out. Why don't you stop this conflict between me and you? You don't want this to drag out for a long time, so why don't you submit to this town's morals? After all, you don't want to be exiled again," Anaeus appeals to her.

"But why can't I be myself? Why can't I stay in this town and be myself as well?" Serena answers Anaeus's question with her own.

"Because you will be exiled if you don't submit," Anaeus retorts sternly.

"All I've been told all my life is to submit, submit, submit. Well, what if I don't want to submit to anyone? I want to be independent instead. I want to be independent from you, independent from this town. If the Christian life is all about the rules, I don't to be a part of it," Serena yells as years of frustration boil over.

"Then you will get your wish," Anaeus remarks sternly but softly. He marches away, leaving Serena to wonder whether she has said too much.

People steadily file into the sanctuary. They remind Serena of the stream in her canyon. The first trial's attendance had felt like an ordinary ladies' society meeting where nobody except the essential staff shows up. However, on this occasion, every resident—either predicting a conflicting battle of legal wits or another brutal punishment for the condemned criminal—has shown up.

The whole village is excitedly anticipating this trial like the Fourth of July's firework show. Serena folds her hands in her lap.

Not a muscle moves from its selected spot. The raucous atmosphere closes around her like a constrictor's coils. She feels unmovable. But Serena does not fight alone. Her mind reflects on the friendship she has made with Jack Irving. So, she stares confidently into the face of her troubles and degrades them with her internal laughter.

Once the residents are seated, Anaeus steps up and Serena pays as much attention to him as she would give in a lecture on wholesome feminine values. Anaeus faces the Owls and delivers his speech.

"You have heard the arguments concerning Serena that resulted in her exile three weeks ago." He pauses to take a deep breath. "The defendant here was convicted of conspiracy to commit mischief, causing discord, and harboring sinful relics. Now she is attempting to reenter this town without fully completing her sentence. The Bible clearly states in multiple places that those guilty of wrongdoing shall be punished. Therefore, I motion for immediate exile of the defendant."

Anaeus faces the crowd as he reaches his conclusion. Meanwhile, Serena stands up, ready to defend herself against Anaeus's accusations. Taking a great breath, she begins.

"It is true that you previously heard these charges and that I was convicted as well, but what you do not know is that these accusations are false."

Serena halts, allowing her words to take effect. The congregation is shocked, and ripples of gossip travel through the pews. Anaeus's eyes grow wide in both shock and dread. The Owls' faces harden, and their eyes narrow. How could Serena have known? Yet she is poised to reveal all Anaeus's foolish deeds, and anyone involved with him will not leave unscathed.

Serena continues, "It was Anaeus who conspired against me and exiled me on made-up charges because I don't fit his definition of what a woman should be. Toby was simply a front so that Anaeus didn't need to challenge me."

Anaeus knows his position is deteriorating. Recovering from his initial shock, he tries to salvage his argument. His concentration narrows, as his reputation is now in danger. After a brief moment of thought, Anaeus attempts to regain the advantage in this trial.

"These are some strong words, but how could you have known in the first place?"

"Because I listened in on your conversation that night. Toby saw it happen and brought it up in the last trial. Pastor Titus, I believe you were the one to question Toby about it," Serena relies. She believes Anaeus is struggling. Now all she must do is respond to his questions and she will win the trial, or at least public support.

"All right," Anaeus exclaims. "But why now at this trial? Why did you not speak up at the last trial? You might have been acquitted. I think that with all that time in the forest, you had a lot of time to think and rehearse this hoax." His tenacious attack upon her moral high ground appears to catch her by surprise.

"What? I—No! I am not making this up!" Serena says. She can feel her advantage over Anaeus slipping away. She shakes her head, becoming disoriented by Anaeus's statements. "I have no reason to lie, and you have every reason to hide the truth." She speaks more toward the crowd or anyone who will hear her.

"Because you want revenge over those who found you guilty. However, you're more guilty than ever before. This might have been your plan all along. Act suspicious until someone like Toby denounces you and we exile you. However, you want to be exiled so that you can feel justified when you reenter this court. You will then say that the people who denounced you were liars and dishonor us all. Quite an elaborate design, but now it is foiled, and you will be punished for your crimes," Anaeus argues.

Upon hearing this, Mary steps out from the interested audience, which has been utterly silent, as if a pastor were preaching. She marches irately down the aisle to the defendant box.

She speaks loudly to the quiet crowd. "I refuse to have myself quoted in this witch hunt. The last trial was nothing but a farce. Anaeus approached Toby and gave Toby the leadership that Toby coveted. Anaeus is behind Serena's denouncement, trial, and exile."

Ripples of disturbed gossip travel through the audience as the Owls' faces beseech Serena for mercy. Serena briefly reflects on her defense. It may not have been an oratory masterpiece worthy enshrinement in the cannon of speeches, but it had conveyed the idea she wanted portrayed. If the Owls declare her guilty, the outcry will force them to retire. Even if an exile is pronounced, Serena will go knowing she will fight until every trick is completely exhausted. However, she does not want Mary to get the final word.

"Anaeus, I don't understand why you target me when there are so many other people who also want to be free from your rules. Is it because of my mom's free spirit?"

"Your mother had a sinful sprit, not a free one. Don't deny this, everyone here knows and you are the proof." Anaeus rumbles, "Your mother would go into the forest to commit heinous sins. I did not want you to repeat your mother's mistakes, and I wanted to watch over you."

Serena feels taken aback. She had always thought that Anaeus just wanted to squelch her fun. Although she has many questions, words fail her.

At length, Gregory clears his throat. "Is that all you have to say?" he asks, masking his unnerved demeanor.

"Yes, it is," Serena says. She takes her seat to wait for another term in exile. She prepares herself for that to be the outcome of her second hearing.

"The jury will adjourn for the time being," Gregory declares, and the Owls begin to rise from the benches where they have been sitting for the hearing. Now the steadiness of their countenance has deserted them like a rogue soldier.

Anaeus subtly leans into Gregory's ear, and something passes between them that Serena can't understand. The Owls leave the stage to carry out their duty. Their decisions influence many. As they cumbersomely file out of their pews, Titus's eyes catch Serena's and he faintly winks at her. That makes Serena feel uneasy. What can it mean?

Serena sits in her box for an eternity. She feels years slip by.

Jack walks up and whispers, "Josiah has reported that the Owls seem to be having a fight in there."

"What type of fight?" Serena whispers back. She thinks an unusual development is unfolding. She had expected to be wandering in the forest again by now.

"I don't know, but Josiah says that it's really loud. The Owls were really yelling at someone," Jack replies, excited.

Serena sits back and puts a hand to her forehead, dazed, so Jack leaves her with her thoughts. Eventually, the Owls wearily file from wherever they went when they discussed these hearings. Serena notices that every suit has undergone severe ruffling. Every Owl, except for Anaeus, catches Serena's flabbergasted gaze this time. Then Titus delivers the verdict.

"After much heated deliberation," Titus shouts in a voice that croaks like a frog, "we declare the defendant innocent of all original crimes, thus making recent crimes illegitimate. Court dismissed!"

The crowd erupts in a raucous, confusing mixture of cheers and boos. Serena leans into the chair in her box, relieved that the fight is finally over. She has won. She can stay in Christville. Serena smiles, knowing that she can never lose.

She looks into the crowd. Standing in the front row, Jack smiles uncontrollably. His football team cheers as if they all have received full academic scholarships to Alabama University's football team. Then, looking into the pews, she spots Jack's mother, Mariah, sitting with some of her friends from the ladies' society. They do not cheer, but they do not voice their disapproval. Instead, Mariah remains composed and attentive. Serena can guess that Mariah wanted her to be exiled but for reasons that cannot be deciphered at the present moment. Serena turns her attention back to the whooping football team. She strolls out of the box and to Jack's side. The pair happily embrace.

"We won. We have finally won," whispers an awestruck Jack to his protector.

"Cherish it. Celebrate it. We did this," Serena speaks in a voice that only Jack can hear.

The pair navigate the crowd and exit the church. The throng is too preoccupied to notice their exit.

That evening, Serena hears the football team running throughout the town, whooping like a band of Indians. They play one of the best football games of the year before disappearing into the forest and to the bridge over the river for a week-long camping trip. Everyone gathers their emergency camping supplies from their hiding places. Perceval steals the "Most Creative Hiding Spot" award when he laboriously clambers underneath the bridge, claiming he got the idea from Lawrence. However, everyone ultimately ignores him, and they go camping.

CHAPTER 27

# THE AFTERMATH

Serena and Jack lie next to each other, facing the stars on one edge of the swimming hole. The camping trip has lasted for three days. Sheldon and Annemarie and several other parents come out to enjoy the forest and take shifts to watch everyone.

Serena and Jack happily stare into the glorious night sky. The moon disappears from its normal place, replaced by the Milky Way with every gem of its God-made glory. Meanwhile, the flames of the campfires gradually descend into glowing coals and ashes. The football team are in various stages of sleeping, dozing, quietly conversing, or stargazing like Jack and Serena. A minority of swimmers splash around in the dark swimming hole. The splashes echo across the canyon, along with laughter from the few swimming.

Jack and Serena are rarely seen apart during the entire trip. Whether fishing, swimming, or simply walking the paths, the couple enjoy each other's company. The entire football team feels overjoyed nonetheless, and every protector is subsequently invited. For a while, neither Jack nor Serena speaks.

Then Serena punctures the silence. "Jack, I think we should keep our friendship to a minimum. It's not that I don't love being around you, but I've been thinking. I think if we don't talk about this now, we could end up like Toby and Mary. Just because we're Christians doesn't mean we are immune to whatever mess they got themselves into, and I don't want to have to cope with that."

"It sounds like your mind is making up worst case scenarios. Do you really think I'm going to become like Toby? That guy became a predator, but now he's dead. Everything is fine, Serena."

Serena is silent for a few moments as she attempts to select the correct words. "You're probably right about that, Jack. I just got to thinking that Toby's relationship with Mary ended with Mary feeling like her dress could be ripped at any second, and mine was nearly shredded. So, I think we should only hang out in groups of friends. That will keep us both safe."

"You're probably right. We can hang out at the parties and games and such. We enjoy our company, but let's keep it in groups. We need to guard our reputations."

The conversation dies out, and the pair continue to contemplate the magnificent starry night sky.

At length, Jack breaks the starlit stillness. "Life is not just about following directions, checking the boxes, and fretting about whether or not something is legal. You can follow all the Christian rules or morality, but if you don't experience the relationship with God, you have to ask yourself why you are doing all this."

Serena contemplates this new thought. "I know. I should know. My life has been a long scenario of broken rules, failed systems, and an exile to go along with them, but many people live their lives according to a moral code of laws that tell them what they should and should not do. I mean, look at Toby. He followed all the rules and look at the monster he became. Rules are nothing. If God doesn't change you though a relationship with him, it's easy to just be a fake."

Once again, the conversation quiets. Jack sighs. "Do you think God controlled recent events?"

"The Bible says God is always in control. Besides, I always thought that if God could make the world in seven days, he should be able to control it. Furthermore, the Bible bears further witness to his continued sovereignty. But I have to admit, this summer was very nerve-racking and unexpected," Serena says.

"For sure. Come on, Serena. Let's go."

Jack heaves himself up and helps Serena to her feet. They stride over to the group of sleeping bags that litter one side of the dark clearing. After Jack joins the boys, Serena finds her own sleeping bag next to a slumbering Sarah. She turns down the lantern and promptly falls asleep. This summer has been an adventure.

Printed in the United States
by Baker & Taylor Publisher Services